Brandon's Journey East and West

A Novel by Adam Kovynia

Copyright © 2018 by Adam Kovynia

All rights reserved

Cover art by Adam Kovynia

ISBN

978-0-578-43613-5

Dedication

For those who purchased a copy of my first book, Max's Modern-Day Philosophy. Your purchase makes a difference in my life.

Part One

Chapter 1

That place I want to be

"I'll have a gin and tonic please," I yelled to the bartender. I yelled only because he wouldn't have heard me otherwise. It's all part of the excitement in the bar scene. I hadn't had a gin and tonic in ages, but I saw someone drinking one in a movie the other day and it struck a chord with me. I thought about this while I reached into my pocket and handed the bartender the cash leaving a single one-dollar bill on the counter as a tip.

"Thanks!" he yelled out with a smile then moved onto the next person.

I walked towards the round tables and saw some couples sitting there while some tables were completely empty. Yet the bar was crowded enough anyways. It was because people were congregating near the rock band. They were good. I enjoyed the sound of their music in the background as I walked around the place. Brick walls along one side and some vintage photos along the next wall I passed. Glowing neon signs here and there emitted a cool electric ambience. I didn't want to sit down at a table because I was by myself, so I just kept strolling throughout the bar. A guy was walking towards me rather quickly without paying much attention then bumped shoulders with me saying "sorry."

It was OK; crowded bars are kind of fun for me anyhow. It reminded me of a time going back fifteen years at least. *Oh God, was it that long ago?* I was in Hartford at a club which surely does not exist by the same name now, and I was under twenty-one but legally I was ok to enter since it was an eighteen-plus night. Being there with older cousins made it easy enough to sip on some cocktails. It was crowded that night. Beyond crowded and I was making my way through the sea of people when a girl behind me, likely about the same age as me, was so close to me that we somehow managed to hold hands suddenly. Now I don't know if it was her or I that initiated it, but we continued holding hands and making our way through the people for maybe half a minute until I let go of her hand. During the time our hands were entwined, I glanced back to look at her once. She looked happy in that split second. It was a moment of excitement and maybe awkwardness under the surface. It's likely we both accidently reached for each other's hands at the same time. That's what it felt like anyways, but some people say *there are no accidents in life*. Maybe I should not have let go of her hand. Maybe I should have asked for her name or spent some time with her. It could have led to a kiss for all I know.

Back to the present moment. I walked through a narrow passageway where there was a large window looking out onto the parking lot in the backside of the bar. I stood there to glance at the outdoors in the dark. Someone tapped me on my right shoulder. "What's your name?" she asked with her eyes opened slightly wider than normal. She has curly blonde hair and looks cute with a tank top on.

"I'm Brandon."

"I like that name."

"I'm named after one of my grandparents from Ireland."

"Oh yeah? I'm Irish myself, well mostly."

"That's nice and same here, I'm also mostly Irish," I responded.

She just kept looking at me and our eyes caught each other's. It was nice because she was so damn cute and unexpected as well. Maybe she didn't know what to say next. I glanced down at her jeans. They were tight blue jeans with some rips in them. She also had a pair of sandals on. What can I say; she looks like she fit right in at this place.

"I'm going to head over to the bathroom; I'll be right back," she stated.

"I'll be right here."

I didn't know what else to do but sit in the big blue arm chair situated in the corner by the massive window I was standing at. It was perfect for me as it only seated one as opposed to those round tables I mentioned earlier which had room for two or three. I plopped down in the blue chair, sinking into it comfortably. I felt reassured that this cute lady was talking to me.

She returned from the ladies' room and I got up while she was walking my way. I returned to that large window and pointed my right finger out in the direction of the street.

"I like this small-town feel," I said.

"Yeah, you can only take so much of a place like Hartford, right?" she responded.

"Exactly, and the fact that this place is directly in a neighborhood is what makes it a little bit unique. I mean, there are bars in neighborhoods in Connecticut, don't get me wrong but some of them are a bit seedy and this place is pretty legit."

"It's not fancy but it's got a cool atmosphere," she said.

"Yes, exactly what I was thinking. So, what's *your* name?" I realized I didn't ask her earlier.

"Summer."

"Summer, that's a great name."

That name completely described her from head to toe. And the fact that it was actually summertime made it that much more appropriate.

"What are you drinking?" She looked over and peered into my glass. This woman is kind of forward, but I liked it. In truth she really wasn't my type because she seemed much more of a hippie and I was more of a square for lack of a better word. "You're not drinking anything." Only ice remained in my cup and I'd just occasionally shuffle around the ice by shaking the cup back and forth taking a little sip of ice water.

"I was drinking gin and tonic. Would you like to take a shot with me? It's on me," I offered.

"Um yeah, sure. Irish whiskey or something different?"

"Well, I'd actually prefer spiced rum. Nothing against Irish whiskey but rum and a beer would be good."

"Right on, sounds good," she said.

We walked over to the bar and she still had about a fourth of a beer in her pint glass, so she tilted back her head and downed the rest of it then slammed it on the counter which caused a loud enough noise to make a few people turn their heads in our direction.

I turned over in bed now laying on my back and opened my eyes. *What an amazing dream,* I thought to myself. I concentrated on remembering everything I could about it and got up to look out the window of my apartment to see where that noise came from. Was it in my imagination or was there a loud bang which translated into a pint glass being slammed down on a counter in a mysterious bar during my dream? And by a cute looking hippie chick with bright blonde hair. Hmmm....I don't know. I looked through the window more carefully and discovered nothing else besides the somewhat urban looking street in New Britain where I rented my one-bedroom apartment. I continued to glance out the window of the high-rise, looking into the dark night. Street lights illuminated the quiet road. A raccoon hurried by. Interesting I thought, *you don't see that every day.*

I sat back down in bed then reached over to my nightstand to take a drink from a bottle of water. I took a couple of deep breaths and laid back down in bed, so I could sleep some more.

Tomorrow would be my last day at the store and my life was kind of in limbo now.

Chapter 2

The beginning of something new

It would be the beginning of something new, but what? I took a shower and enjoyed using one of those jumbo-sized soaps, scented sea breeze. I also washed my hair with a fancy shampoo I saw on a 90s drama TV series. At first glance I didn't know if it was an actual product or just something made up for the show, but after googling it, I was able to buy a bottle online. Aromatherapy can be a powerful force, you know.

I ran out the door and walked towards my car. A couple was having an argument next to their car in the parking lot of the apartment complex. The woman was very rough around the edges in her tone of voice and although I had no clue what they were really arguing about or even who they were, I felt glad I wasn't involved with problems like that at the moment. I pulled out of the parking lot, and around the corner I hopped onto 9 North for several minutes while flipping through radio stations. Typical raunchy morning talk radio but I get a kick out of it nonetheless. I got onto Route 10 which is a rather scenic drive when you're in Farmington and Avon, Connecticut. Beyond that, going north towards Massachusetts, it's also quite beautiful but my stop was in Avon. A rather ideal town located more or less slightly north of the geographic center of Connecticut and surrounded by other pleasant and well-off towns. I liked it here in Avon where my store was. I even considered moving here to an apartment but never got around to it. I was close enough to work living in New Britain, otherwise known as the *Hardware City* or *Hard Hittin'* and the cost of living was cheaper, so I stayed. Plus, before I started managing the store in Avon, I was at the Westfarms mall up until they phased out that location and now, well now they are shutting down my current store. Across the nation they are closing down fifty percent of all our stores. We were one of the most popular clothing lines in America during the late 80s and early 90s. You know that whole surfer neon beach type of look? That was one of the popular styles back around that era and our store sold that type of look along with some affordable jewelry, colognes, perfumes and accessories for men and women. At one point we even had a magazine for sale that was short lived in the grand scheme of things, but you can find copies for sale on eBay! High-schoolers and college kids especially were our biggest target. The store made a comeback in the late 90s especially 1998. As time went on, we've just sort of maintained up until the last couple of years and now so many of our stores are shutting down. We're not in all fifty states but we're a well-known name. Back in the early 90s I was in elementary school and I wouldn't have ever figured someday I'd be an assistant manager at a trendy store like this. I figured I'd be lucky if I could fit into any of their clothes in the first place. I was considerably overweight. But it was the whole image that was sold along with the clothes that probably made an impression on me back then. TV stars were wearing it, people I saw here and there in the general public as well of course. It was a dream for me to one day look different, feel different and be a whole new person really.

"Hi Jane. Good morning," I said once I walked halfway into the store.

"Here's the list, Brandon. Take your time." She handed me a checklist of things I would complete today on my final day at work. Taking down clothes off the shelves, storing it away in boxes for starters and a variety of other tasks. The store was not open to customers anymore, yet it would take more than just today to complete all the work needed to be done. But they only needed me today. After that, the rest of the staff would finish up for I'd say at least the rest of the week. Today was Monday.

Jane was *sexy*. Jane was *single*. Jane was Japanese-American and older than me. I'm thirty-five years old and she is thirty-nine. I can't say that I knew all her personal life details, yet I knew she wasn't married. Ironically, I got most of my information about her through your daily gossip that all of us coworkers did together. It's not that we gossip about her more but that we just plain gossip about anybody or anything. And when I'm not there, sure, they gossip about me, why not?

"I'm going to miss you Brandon," Jane said with a tear in her eye. Maybe it wasn't a tear *exactly*, but I could kind of sense it was how she felt. I could see it in her eyes. "I'm not just saying that because I'm your manager. Sure, yeah, I will say something like this to everyone who will leave here in the upcoming week but you're perfect Brandon. You're always here, you're never calling out sick. You've made this place what it is." And now she did shed a tear. I couldn't believe she was actually crying over me for a couple of seconds at least.

I did what I never did before. I reached in to give her a hug. I figured, why not? It was my last day and under the circumstances it made sense. She was the general manager, so I worked directly under her as assistant manager and then we had a couple more who were part of the leadership team. That's the main reason why I didn't ever realistically consider dating her. Plain and simple: it was against the rules as it is in most all places of employment. I did, however, date another associate I worked with back at Westfarms mall but that was before I was in management, so it was completely appropriate so long as it didn't cause problems or interfere with the job in other words. Yet at our current store I did go out to lunch, dinner and the bar with coworkers. Still it wasn't considered dating although a little flirtation went on amongst coworkers.

I got to work on my checklist and started sorting through all the apparel. In the background, music played as it always did in the store. The same songs were on rotation. Then I stopped for a moment, put down the tee shirt I had folded in my hands, and realized this was the last day I'd listen to these songs in this store. Between this store and the previous one at the mall, it's been just over a decade that I've worked for this company. I continued folding. I felt a hand on my right shoulder gently. I wondered who it could be as I turned my head to the right. It was Karen. She was a student at University of Hartford studying Illustration on her sixth year. She'd been taking classes part time for the past couple of years as she needed to supplement her income and just couldn't afford to keep attending full time.

"Hi Karen," I said.

"Hey," she said.

I'm going to miss this place. I'd thought a lot about life in these past several years. Take

Karen for instance. She'd been here before I got to this location and I'd shown her some of my drawings I'd done back in high school. I'd taken every art class offered back then and I'd always had a talent since as early as second grade or so. One drawing I'd done of Nicole Kidman came out surprisingly well and people could see the likeness. She was impressed, and I think she'd also taken an interest in me looks wise. She has kind of this punk rock thing going on which made me sort of wonder why she'd work at a store like this which had a bit more of a preppy look, yet it worked for her still. We were not quite the Gap, or American Eagle. We were like a cross between Abercrombie and OP and maybe a little Eddie Bauer. Hey, you've got to remember we've been around forever and we were sort of our own thing. She was petite, and the clothes looked good on her. She had her tattoos and earrings-lots of them. I'd realized that if I'd taken classes like she'd had in college, I'd easily be as able to make works of art as good as the next student, but I didn't go that route. In my case I was dissuaded from it by family, so instead I did a year and a half of full time study at one of the state universities. The cost was very reasonable, and it was local, so I just commuted from home while living with parents. But I couldn't stand it. Advertising was my major yet just after a year and a half of attending courses, I was mentally burnt out and pretty much miserable there. I felt just like a number and not a person plus I always told myself one day I'd study at a private college in Vermont. Well, that never happened and I'm halfway through my thirties now.

I glanced down at my watch and realized I'd been here for three hours and was starting to feel hungry. I heard some tables being shuffled around. "Lunch is here!" Jane yelled out. Jane ordered pizza from the best shop in town. She got my favorite: eggplant and broccoli. Another large pizza was half cheese and half peperoni. Chicken wings and blue cheese dressing. Carrots and celery on the side. In addition to that, large bottles of soda. If that wasn't enough Jane ordered sushi from a trendy new Japanese restaurant down the road. I still never ate there so here was my chance to try the vegetable roll. She'd also ordered a special blend of cherry flavored green tea which she prepared in the back. Jane appeared from the back office and set down fancy ceramic tea cups along with a pot of the prepared tea. She asked me if I'd like a cup.

Jane poured the hot tea into the fancy cups for us both, steam rising all around. She looked at me and our eyes met. This time it was different than ever before. Was there something in the way she looked at me that held some kind of meaning? We brought our tea cups together giving off a subtle clinking sound as we both said "cheers." I took a sip and savored the flavor. I walked over to the table in the center of the room and got myself a plate. I tried the vegetable sushi. She knew I was a vegetarian so accordingly she got what I could eat and some fish for the rest of the staff. I looked over at the pizza again and thought about how she ordered my favorite toppings without asking me first what I wanted. I felt it could have been a sign and her way of saying *I know what he likes, I'll surprise him with getting it.* Earlier Karen said *she'd miss this place,* but Jane has said to me *I'm going to miss you.* Hmmm…Sometimes I wondered if Jane liked me more than just as a coworker. She was totally professional but not fake at all. She just did her job and knew it would be inappropriate to cross the line. But who really knows? This is all speculation. I've done this all my life. Speculate about different things.

Speaking of appropriateness, or lack thereof, Karen had "crossed the line" so to speak at her on-campus apartment with me one night about three years ago. I'll never forget it. Brad was there with us. He'd been an associate at the store back then. There was also Michelle, she'd been with us too. She still works with us, now a part-timer. We'd all been invited to go out and party with Karen at the university. Really everyone at the store was invited but the rest of the staff had other engagements. The night wore down, Brad and Michelle headed home, and I was getting into my car when Karen texted me asking if I wanted to come up and watch a movie with her. She conveniently mentioned she'd found a bottle of rum, unopened, and she'd make us some rum and cokes. If I wanted to, I could stay over and use her roommate's bed. She was away for the weekend back home in Jersey. Hmmm… *what to do*, I thought. Was it worth risking my job over having a relationship of sorts with her *or* was it that she just wanted someone to *hang out* with? So, I did go up and we started watching a comedy with Ben Stiller and Jennifer Aniston called *Along Came Polly*. I was enjoying my rum and coke, so was she. I glanced over at her after I took a sip to see Karen was slurping the sweet drink then smiled while I could hear the ice crackling in her teeth next. Suddenly she scooted over closer to me on the couch. We were already sitting close together. Now it was to the degree that our bodies were rubbing up against each other. I got excited about that right away. I felt flattered. And I think the thing which surprised me the most was that I was a really a clean-cut kind of guy, so I figured she wouldn't go for my type. Keep in mind how I grew up being ostracized for my weight and all. Looking back on it I realized how Karen and I both had the artistic mindset and we did work together after all. So, we had things in common in that respect. There's always that saying *opposites attract* as well let's not forget. Clearly, she was attracted to me. I found her eyes beautiful. They were hazel and her hair, although streaked with a type of punk rock red, was still looking sexy to me. You see, I go for the conservative type yet really, I'm attracted to all types pretty much on some level. Then it happened. She looked over at me while I was still focused on the movie. I noticed it out of the corner of my eyes. So, then I turned my head and looked at her. She was purposefully looking at me. Directly in my eyes. Karen put her hand on my face; I smelled the delicate fragrance of her perfume. My heart raced, and I took a breath through my mouth. Next, she tilted her head a bit then kissed me. It was a pleasant soft gentle kiss that would go down in my memory banks forever. Then I pulled my head back for a second. Next, I leaned into her and kissed her back. This time our tongues were intertwined. It lasted for a good twenty seconds. "I have to go Karen," I told her.

"OK. Is it because you're my manager and you don't want to get in trouble for anything?" she asked.

"Yes, that's why," I said levelly.

"I won't say anything to anyone and you don't say anything to anyone and we'll just be friends and leave it at that," she suggested.

"OK, good, so I'll just head home now?"

"I'm OK with that," she said.

I got up and made sure I had my keys, wallet, and cell phone. I felt a little nervous. As I approached the door, I turned and looked at her on the couch. "Karen."

"Yes?"

"I really liked that kiss. I mean I really liked it."

"So, did I, Brandon." I turned the door handle. "Wait, Brandon." She put her open hand to her mouth and kissed it then blew the kiss in my direction.

"Thank you. Good night," I said as I left. And that was it. That was really it. After that we didn't talk about it or do anything other than go out as a group of coworkers now and then plus work together. It was because of my integrity. Not to toot my own horn or anything but really, I felt lucky enough to have this job and I wanted to do the right thing.

I grabbed myself a couple slices of broccoli and eggplant pizza and leaned against the counter where the register was in the far left side of the store. I drank a cold seltzer along with it and still had my tea on the counter. After I finished eating I'd decided to refill my tea and noticed Jane was off on the phone by the other register. I walked around the store with my tea leisurely. Samantha was there having a slice of cake. "Chinese tea, huh?" she asked.

"Well, actually it's Japanese. I read the label and Jane is Japanese you know?" I responded.

"Oh really, I didn't know. You like her, don't you?" she said a little louder than she probably should have. Every employee in the store turned their head in our direction.

"Yes!" I responded without thinking of anyone hearing me. I looked over and saw Karen watching us then I looked over at Jane still on the phone but looking right at me all the while. I don't know that she heard me say the word "yes" or if she knew what it pertained to. I also don't know what possessed me to just say that I liked her but then again what possessed Samantha to ask me like that? It was the final week of this store's existence in this location plus we were already closed to customers. For all intents and purposes, we might as well do whatever we please. Jane will be moving on to another location and I will soon enough figure out something else to do with my life. This whole being laid off thing is new to me and it came so suddenly. I'm getting paid a healthy chunk of money for being laid off as part of an agreement with the store but that won't last me long.

It's pretty strange. I'm connected to most of the associates here on social media including Jane. But her Facebook page is very bare. Hardly more than a couple photos of her and she never posts anything. I suppose it's just sort of a placeholder if you will. Like a way to keep track of everyone's birthday and have personal references. There's more information regarding her resume online than information on her Facebook. But that's ok. I basically cherish those few photos of her I see online. OK so yes, I *do* like her.

"Brandon, do you have the time?" Michelle called over to me from a few feet away. She was on a ladder bringing down women's jeans.

"3:57," I responded.

"You could have just said four."

"OK, OK, whatever. Where's Jane? I'm about ready to head out after another hour."

"She's gone. She left."

"For the day? Maybe she ran to the bank or something?"

Michelle climbed down from the ladder quickly and walked over to me. She put her hand on my back for a second. "You *do* really like her, don't you?"

I kept a professional mindset and didn't want to jeopardize anything.

"You know how lately for the past year you've been talking about your odd plan to travel cross-country to Nebraska?" Michelle asked.

"Yeah."

"The other day when you were off work, it was slow. Real slow. No wonder we're going out of business. Well, half our stores are anyways. We were all congregating around the main cash register up front and we were like asking each other trivia questions and telling jokes. It was nice. So, Jane asks where did Johnny Carson grow up? And you know Mike was here, and he doesn't even know who Johnny Carson was, but we explained to him that he's like the equivalent of Jimmy Fallon or a Jay Leno you know? So, nobody guessed it and she said, Nebraska!"

"OK, I get it so she's thinking about me and she knows that I have this so-called odd idea about moving there," I responded.

"Yeah, but that's not all Brandon. Jane elaborated about it afterwards. Like saying how Nebraska looks like a nice place to settle down."

"Really?"

"Yeah, like when we were making jokes about how you want to go there. Seriously it's just because it seems so different from here in Connecticut plus typically people here move down to Florida or the Carolinas more often. Maybe California like my neighbor did, let's say, but Nebraska is just an out of left field choice, right?"

"Sure, so you guys brought me up in conversation?"

"Yeah basically and Jane is telling us about Lake McConaughy and how it's like the beach of Nebraska since it's a land locked state and doesn't have an ocean, so you've got this lake which looks a lot like the beach does here in Connecticut. If you look at some of the photos, you've got people driving their cars up on the sand and all that stuff," Michelle said.

"Hmmm." It got me thinking. Maybe Jane did really think about me. After all, why was she single and at *her* age? Also, I have never been married, but I'd dated enough. "Michelle, do you think that it was OK for me to date customers who came in here over the years?"

"You're fine by doing that. They come in here to shop, they see a good-looking guy like you or say Brad when he *was* here, they flirt. It's quite honestly a good way to meet people. I've done it myself."

"Yeah….hmm. Why do you think Jane never said anything much about my dating life?"

"She likes you and that's why. She didn't want to piss you off and become your enemy by telling you what you should or shouldn't do. But you didn't hear it from me."

I ran my fingers through my hair and stopped to think about everything. A little while longer and I'd be done for the day. Done forever here at this store.

Chapter 3

Let's go east

When I left work that day, my final day, I walked out into the parking lot and thought to myself: *I really want to make love to Jane. Passionately.* I'm not saying it will ever happen, but it was just a thought. And I did never see her again that day. So, she had gone home without saying anything to me. I got on social media and chatted with Karen that night to ask her. Karen said Jane told everyone goodbye as she headed out the door for the day while I was using the restroom. Karen or the rest of the staff had forgotten to tell me this earlier I suppose. Well who knows, after all what would Jane want with me anyways?

Just like the popular clothing line that I sold for about a decade was fading out considerably, so was my life. I was getting older by the day. Not married. And ready to start a new chapter in my life, but where? I got tired of living in New Britain. Sick and tired of it. I hadn't always lived there. I'd grown up in the suburbs of another town in Connecticut. New Britain was of course conveniently located to the mall which I worked at plus when I moved locations, Avon was not that far off, twenty some odd minutes was reasonable. But that was all over now. So, who was I? And where would I go?

I put on a pair of sunglasses over my contacts that morning and packed a tote bag with a couple of books-personal memoirs for inspiration. A bottle of water and a large Ziploc bag with almonds, cashews, peanuts, brazil nuts, dates and apricots, all salted. I even sprinkled in roasted soybeans for extra health. You can't go wrong with that extra protein and fiber, plus they're low in fat. When you're a vegetarian anyways, you've got to do what you've got to do. I took a map of Connecticut from my desk drawer and studied it. I'd realized that I'd seldomly went east of the Connecticut River. Sure, there were the two casinos and the Manchester mall which I enjoyed. I liked all of Manchester since they had so many stores and all but beyond that, what else was out there east of the river? I knew it was a lot quieter than other parts of Connecticut. They even called it the "Quiet Corner" in one section. Sure, I'd also been there at a couple of wine tastings with my ex-girlfriends, but the past was the past.

I hopped in my car and flipped through my CD booklet. It held 64 CDs, yet I could hardly find anything to pique my interest. Ughhh…. then I saw it. *Smalltown Poets*. "Aha!" I said out loud. Here was a CD that I'd basically never listened to more than once, and it'd been sitting here for I don't know, a year. It was Jane's CD, but she'd let me borrow it because we were talking music one slow evening at work. The two of us were on alone. I remember looking out the window and seeing the sky gradually turn to twilight then a shade darker and darker until later I glanced out to a pitch-black night. The temperature was pleasant inside and I had a cozy feeling for some reason. Another associate called out "sick," and it was slow enough that we didn't need anyone else to fill in. In truth both her and I probably avoided getting too close to each other because we liked each other so much, secretly, so our relationship was strictly professional. I think it's her level of integrity that made it so. It's like she had a rock-solid discipline in life for doing everything the best she could. As one of our conversations found its way into the topic of music, I told her how I loved the song *Dreams* by Van Halen. Can you believe she'd never heard it? I let her borrow it, the CD *5150* by *Van Halen* and in exchange she'd given me this album by *Smalltown Poets* titled *Third Verse*. A simple folk-art style illustration of the band members graced the cover. I'd never really given it a chance. Nor did I ever return it to her. She hadn't returned the *Van Halen* CD to me either. Come to think of it, we *never* discussed the music we'd exchanged. Yet that evening at work was *special*. It was likely the most pleasant night at work I'd ever had. It felt like a calm and harmonious Wednesday when all was okay with the world. Clearly, we were into each other now that I look back on it. She'd leaned into the table crossing her arms and then resting her chin on top of them, looking at me intently that evening. She was so beautiful. Jane had never paid me a compliment looks wise though, beyond mentioning my clothes fit great on me. But that was her professionalism. Also, I'd never directly told her how beautiful I thought she was. Maybe she'd picked up on how I felt by the way I'd look at her on a couple of occasions. Yet it's not like I stared at her or anything, I'd had more tact than that.

Traveling east basically required I'd go through Hartford on the highway, where I'm coming from anyways. It's a pressure cooker out there dealing with the traffic but what the hell, it's not like I haven't done it a thousand times already by this age. I'd lived in the nutmeg state all my life after all. While I sipped a coffee from my travel mug, I'd put in the *Smalltown Poets* CD. Better late than never; I guess you don't know what you've got till it's gone. That's referring to Jane of course, but the CD, well I suppose I'd have that for the rest of my life. The music was good. I guess I wasn't paying attention the first time I played it last year. It reminds me of *Toad the Wet Sprocket*, which was a phenomenal band as far as I'm concerned. I managed to get in the right lane and follow I84 East towards East Hartford. I glanced down at the CD case because I liked to know what the names of the songs were. Passing through East Hartford I started to see signs for Manchester. I decided to get off at exit 62 which was close to the Buckland Hills Mall.

I positioned myself to get in the right lane and took a right up the hill leading to the mall. I was hungry, so I decided to stop in to get a bag of mini salted pretzels. You know the soft kind you can dip in mustard or cheese sauce. I managed to maintain the same weight for the past three or four years and I didn't want a change in life to throw me off again. I got a side of marinara sauce with a soda water on ice. I slurped the seltzer and grabbed a couple napkins then sat down near the center of the mall on a bench. I loved these pretzels with a passion. I think what threw me off weight wise, a few years ago, was changing stores. I went from working at the mall to transferring to the Avon location. New people, new drive, new scenery, new everything. I got in crisis mode so to speak. Ok that's a bold way of putting it, but subconsciously that's how I felt so I turned to food again. I'd been that way as a little kid, but I didn't really grasp the underpinnings of it all back then. I just knew fast food and soda made me feel good and nobody stepped in to really help me out. I was pretty much hopeless without the help. But once I got to my junior year in high school, a major shift took place. People noticed my transformation. It wasn't until age twenty-two though that I really figured out how to get my body to its *ideal* weight. Food is a powerful drug and alcohol can be used in the same way. Fortunately, I've had the mindset to be in control of it all.

I walked through part of the mall and was offered a massage by a lady working at a kiosk standing by a massage chair. A beautiful bouquet of orchid flowers on the table next to her. I stopped almost hesitating for too long then said, "no thank you, maybe next time."

I felt tempted to buy a book at *Barnes and Noble* but resisted the urge. I'd have to make my money last for a while now as I was technically unemployed. The real truth of the matter was that I needed a change in my life and I didn't attempt to find employment in another one of our clothing stores. Ten years was enough. But they were a good ten years and I'd learned a lot managing a store even if I didn't make it to the top in management. I felt comfortable in the position I was in and I loved the different styles in our clothing line. I was in a groove with my physique. My metabolism was always humming along at a good level because I had a reasonable lifestyle. I'd struggled so much as a kid that it made it all the more sweeter these days to enjoy the body I always wished for in my youth. And with the discount I got working there, I'd been able to buy an overload of apparel. Hence the reason I filled two closets at home in my apartment and countless drawers and shelves. I think the other reason I'd always stayed there is because of the attention I received from the customers. I'd dated them and flirted with them and everything was pretty much copacetic. Life went along smoothly.

When I continued to my car I turned the ignition and took a right out of the mall parking lot heading east. I really wanted to get away from what I was used to, so I figured the fastest way was to get back on 84 East in order to reach the town of Vernon for starters. Then from there I'd be in a whole different section of the state as far as I was concerned. Beyond that region of the state, things got typically more rural and small-town Connecticut. I began to take turns right and left to the point where I completely didn't recognize where I was with the exception of road signs I'd glance at pointing out names of towns, routes, state parks, hospitals, gas stations and such. Some of the towns I didn't even recognize. Jane's CD continued playing and when I got to a song called *Firefly,* it had an effect on me. The song was perfect for this time of year, the dog days of summer, and I was quickly realizing how good of a band the *Smalltown Poets* were. I fell into a groove while driving, a forest of trees on both sides of the road stretched on for a while. After a time, I urgently felt the need to use the bathroom. Where am I going to take a pee out here? In the woods? That's not my style unless it was under the right circumstances anyways and this wasn't one of those circumstances. I did see a nice, fresh looking hotel on my right all of a sudden. This should work just fine. I pulled in and parked off to the side where I could find the closest space. Then I marched towards the front entrance. When I passed through the automatic doors, a burst of cool fresh air relieved me from the oppressive summer heat. I walked towards the front desk clerk, a female, wearing a navy-blue dress and white pearl necklace to contrast. She had bangs, medium brown, almost shoulder length hair, straight. Very straight hair. A megawatt smile on her face.

"Can I just use the bathroom? Would that be alright?"

"OK, but it's going to cost you."

"Oh yeah, how much?"

"Our dishwasher called out sick today sooo….."

"Well, I *am* in need of a job. You see, I am looking…."

"I was only kidding, down the hall to your right."

I trotted to the restroom and relieved myself, washed my hands with the liquid green soap, dried them off, then ran my fingers through my hair, checking to see if everything was in place. I dashed back towards the front desk area and thanked the young woman behind the counter. Glancing at her name tag I read: Cassandra. *Nice name* I thought. "Can I have a business card?" I really only wanted to know which town I was in.

"Sure, we are hiring you know."

"Hmmm." I wasn't in a position to jump at a job right now since I'd been planning to take a few weeks off after I found out I'd be laid off from the clothing store. But the economy has seen better days I suppose, and I didn't want to get stuck without work for too long. I figured I'd ask for the cost of a night here and see how I liked the place.

"How much for one night?"

"I'm not for sale!" she responded jokingly. "Bad joke, bad joke, sorry!"

"Oh, thank God, I thought you might have been serious there and misunderstood what I meant."

"Oh, I know what you meant. We're going for $139 plus tax tonight. Are you a Triple A member? If so you can save about ten percent," she offered.

"As a matter of fact, I am."

I gave her what she asked of me: my driver's license, my debit or credit card, my phone number, and email address.

I got situated in my room and laid back on the bed. Pretty comfortable. I took her business card out of my pocket and looked up at it. Cassandra and then a long Polish last name which I could not pronounce properly. In fact, one grandparent of mine is from Poland but mainly we identify with the Irish side if at all. Maybe it's because the Polish language is a difficult one and I could only learn a few words as hard as I tried one summer when I was a lot younger.

I couldn't resist exercising in the hotel gym yet without much on hand I ventured down to the nearest Walmart to pick up exercise shorts, a pair of PJs, deodorant, swimming trunks and some other basic necessities as not to be the victim of highway robbery in the hotel's convenience store. The drive to the Walmart was much longer than I wanted it to be, especially with the summer heat and bumper to bumper traffic I got stuck in. Road construction…what can you do?

I got back to my room and changed into my exercise attire. I walked past the front desk because I didn't really know where the exercise room was, however, Cassandra was busy talking to someone up front. I realized she still noticed me because as I walked by slowly she kept her gaze on me for a second or two. It was easy enough to find the exercise room on my own. I got on a treadmill and started off jogging at four miles per hour. A decent sized television was set to CNN. I broke a good sweat after about eight minutes. It was hot out. The end of June after all. It felt kind of weird not knowing what I'd be doing on the Fourth of July, but I suppose it didn't really matter. My relatives would give me a hard time about not being married if I'd see them at all. Later I picked up some free weights and worked on my biceps. I'd save my other muscle groups for tomorrow. I had a feeling I'd return to this little gym.

I took the stairs back up to my room, 219. Who the hell needs to take the elevator unless you have some sort of ailment anyways? I flipped on the TV. The Weather Channel predicted some hotter than usual temperatures for the next few days. It was ok with me. Connecticut winters are brutal, so I tend not to complain over heat or humidity for that matter. I switched it to CNN as I was getting hooked on the news after watching it downstairs earlier. I jumped in the shower and briskly washed myself for about five minutes. The soap had a musky scent almost like a men's cologne and the shampoo was pretty typical, but I couldn't really label the scent in any way. I dried off with the large white towel and threw on my new swim trunks, a dark brown colored tank top and a pair of flip flops. Their pool was indoors. I opened the door with my plastic hotel key card and felt a warm mist in the air, which I liked. I slowly inched my way in and stretched out a little in the water. They had some alternative rock music playing through the speakers which I was relishing. Or was it adult contemporary? Sort of a blend of the two genres perhaps. Either way life felt good out here in the town of Pine Creek Village. I wondered if it was actually a town or if the "Village" denoted that it was part of a town. Sort of like a section or place in town, a borough? Did Pine Creek have their own high school? Their own zip code?

I swam leisurely around the pool for a few minutes then leaned my back up against the ledge, resting my body in the refreshing water. I heard the door open and glanced upward turning my head. My eyes fixated on a dark blue one-piece swimsuit. I looked her up and down then realized it was Cassandra from the front desk. She smiled. Next, she walked right down the ladder into the pool without saying a word. Literally nobody else was in the pool. I wondered if the hotel was in a dry spell. The parking lot was less than a quarter full after all.

"Hi Brandon," she said.

"Hi Cassandra!" I was enjoying this. Clearly between that obvious big wink she gave me earlier and now her conveniently being in the pool the same time as me-something was up. Even her flirtatious nature when I first walked in the door to use the bathroom got me thinking.

"You can call me Sandy if you like."

"Is that what your friends call you?"

"Yeah, generally. Speaking of them, we are getting together tonight for a late dinner. The Starlight Restaurant just next door. Lex will be there. Missy, Sam, Frank, uh maybe that's about it. Lex's family owns everything."

"Everything?"

"This hotel, the Starlight, the 'shopping mall,' and some real estate beyond all that."

"Wow."

"Yeah it's all here next door. Like the shopping mall is more of a shopping *center* really. We have a department store and there's an auto parts shop. There's a pharmacy, a little coffeehouse which also serves small bites. You see, we don't have a restaurant in the hotel, so we just send everyone next door for everything they need so it works out," she explained.

"So, I'm thinking of taking you up on that offer. Washing dishes or whatever you have available. I know you were only kidding but, I've been assistant manager for years with this clothing company and they're shutting down half their stores. Long story. I'm out of work and I just feel restless not working. I'm thirty-five years old. It's not like I can just retire."

"Oh, we need you here. Trust me. You saw me at the desk earlier, but I do *everything*. I mean everything. I'm general manager but we've had people come and go and I'm responsible for tying up every loose end here," she explained.

Our conversation went on for the next ten minutes. Who would have predicted that by the end of our time in the pool I'd be one short step away from having a job? So long as I'd be flexible. Very flexible with my hours and my responsibilities. The trade-off was, other than having a job, I'd have a place to live for at least the rest of the year which was a good six months from now. And I wouldn't have to pay for it. I'd be able to stay in room 219 daily. Again, the trade-off might mean I'd be working night shifts or day shifts or anything in between. But how bad could it be since I was already living on property. It's not like I'd have to drive through a New England winter storm just to get to work. So even if the pay was less, I'd have a place to stay rent free not to mention my lease is running out by Mid-July at the high rises in New Britain. Indeed, a new chapter of my life was forming.

And in a strange little town called Pine Creek
Village.

Chapter 4

Hustling all week

Cassandra, or should I say Sandy, handed me a fresh, dry towel as we got out of the pool. She even reached out her hand to help me out of the water. I saw her looking at my body as if I was a delectable piece of cake and she was hungry for dessert. I worked hard to get into shape. The definition and muscle tone I had was well earned and the product of eating sensibly, plus training. I got dressed quickly and jogged down the stairs to her office where we went over paperwork. I printed up my resume and filled out several forms. I couldn't believe it was all happening so fast. I learned that truly this hotel was short staffed. They were beyond short staffed. When she was off in the pool with me, Miguel was covering the front desk and he'd not even been officially given that position. He's the houseperson. His job is to clean the lobby, banquet room, restrooms, do security patrols and so forth. Yet he'd shown an interest in learning the front desk, so he'd picked up enough knowledge to cover the area when needed. But did she really need to leave her post to take a dip in the pool with me? I don't know but she'd more or less casted a spell on me. I didn't want to see her disappear from my life yet.

I'd gotten dressed in a pair of khakis and a buttoned-down checkered shirt. An overall green color to it with some blue and red meshed in. I fixed my hair with a small dollop of this pomade stuff I picked up next door at the department store in the shopping center. The clothes, I'd bought them there also. I figured I'd head back to my apartment in New Britain tomorrow, pack all my stuff and move into here. I was ready for a change. At the most I'd check back on the apartment once a week, but I had to move on with my life. I was tired of the hustle and bustle of city life in New Britain and in contrast Pine Creek Village was quite different. It was different from Avon also. Sure, it was a quiet little town in the middle of nowhere but maybe it was just what I needed. I dashed down the stairs and headed towards the front desk to pick up Cassandra for our dinner with the rest of the gang. She wasn't there but I heard someone sobbing in the distance. I positioned myself so that I could see beyond the front desk and into the back office without making myself conspicuous. I was just at the right angle. It was Sandy crying. I thought for a moment what to do. Then I just walked out the front door. I figured it was none of my business, but it got me concerned at the same time. I stepped outside and felt the hot muggy air. It was around 7:30 at night. I walked towards the Starlight and was approached by a friendly looking guy who reached out his hand. "Brandon??"

I reached out my hand to shake his. "Yes, you're?"

"Sam!" he said with a smile.

OK so Sandy must have let them know to expect me I figured. "Follow me," he said. We walked into the restaurant and were seated at one of those long booths which wrapped around and could hold about seven or more people. Missy I presumed was the dark haired, dark eyed beautiful looking woman with strong, chiseled features sitting in the middle. She was thin and maybe even gaunt, could have been Greek, maybe Italian, really, I didn't know. But it turned out I was right, she was Missy. Then Lex, a blond-haired handsome man dressed casually in a polo shirt and shorts. A firm handshake as he introduced himself. Frank, with short dark somewhat curly hair, a sort of buzz cut. Sam was married but his wife couldn't make it. Lex was single and lived in his family's guest house. Indeed, it was true, they owned everything on this plaza and more.

We got to order our food and luckily, they had a veggie bean burger on the menu. I splurged by getting fries and ketchup on the side. Lettuce, tomato, mayo, pickles on a sesame seed bun. It was good. I even had a diet cola on ice to wash it down, which I rarely do.

"Listen guys, I just started work at the hotel next door, but I couldn't get in touch with Cassandra, Sandy…I know she was supposed to be joining us. She was probably tied up or something. I can call her," I offered.

Lex looked up from his food and placed his hand on top of Sam's forearm as if to stop him from saying anything. It's like the motion was non-verbally suggesting to Sam: *I got this.*

Then Lex said, "Sandy is going to have to cover the desk, Brandon."

"Really? But she said she'd eat with us?"

"Miguel went home sick," Lex said.

"I saw Miguel earlier, Sandy explained to me he's the houseperson but is only in training for the front desk so far. Don't you guys have more people Lex? You're the owner, right?" I asked wondering if my question was a little bold. Still I operated on instinct and years of managerial experience.

"My family owns the Hotel, but we don't manage it. Yeah, we're there every couple of days to check up on things but Sandy is holding down the fort, she's the general manager after all. We've had some bad luck with employees lately. We've got a few and the housekeeping team is a really strong asset but when it comes to the front desk, people just keep quitting plus it's her responsibility to schedule properly. You can't just let people have time off whenever they want it," Lex explained.

"I see, well I'm sure I'll be able to help out a bit there."

After our meals were finished we headed across town to the only real bar which was also reasonably OK looking. Hell, it was fun. Basically, a sports bar, small place but not tiny and it was packed, for a weekday anyhow. I was getting to know about this little town of Pine Creek Village. Frank bought me a shot of ice cold Jägermeister and following that a pint of Sam Adam's Boston Lager. I was having a great time. I was elated. There's that weird feeling. I've gotten it before at least a couple times in life. You're around a whole new set of people and stop to ponder it. Just a little while ago I didn't know any of these people and now they'd suddenly become a familiar fixture in my life. That's the feeling I'd get when I'd start dating someone new and hang out with her family or friends. But these guys are not only brand new to me, this town is as well, so it's a little weird but exciting all at the same time. I felt bad about Sandy. Real bad. In my mind I heard her sobbing. I didn't even call her to check up after that. But she is at work after all.

Back to my conversation with Frank… I realized he'd once worked at the hotel but hardly lasted six weeks. The job wasn't for him he'd said. "Population 26,500," Frank said about the size of Pine Creek Village. I nodded to show interest. "And the high school? Smallest in Connecticut." He'd attended, class of 2001 I'd learned from him later in conversation. Occasionally we'd glance over at the women walking by.

Lex had ordered us taxis to get back to the shopping center. The bar was a good ten-minute drive and I'd felt better about not having to drive while drinking. He was generous. He was rich.

In the morning I felt surprisingly refreshed. I woke up not remembering where the hell I was but that always happens staying somewhere out of the norm. I got showered and headed downstairs. I had a couple more papers to sign. Company handbook and guidelines, legalese, you know all that nonsense. Sandy had explained to me that khakis or dress pants were A-OK. A shirt and tie otherwise a buttoned-down shirt with sweater over it were just fine regarding dress code. It would be a long day. Training, training, and more training.

The next day I worked with a part timer named Ralph. An older guy who holds an additional part time job at the town historical center plus numerous hobbies on the side such as bird watching, building model airplanes and cars, and collecting coins and stamps to name a few. He would serve to be someone I'd like to keep in contact with in the long run. A nice man, somewhat of a mentor to me perhaps. He'd trained me good. Real good. Patience was a forte of his.

The following day Maxine was working with me, another part timer. She's a mom to two kids and married to Jonathan who taught at a middle school. I was quickly realizing I'd found a good way to learn about this little town and start a brand-new life. Throughout the day Sandy was swinging by and placing her hand on me along that area between the back of the neck and the shoulders. It felt nice and her hand was warm. She'd promised me twice throughout this day that as long as I stuck with it, she'd make it worth my while. At one point she'd said she'd have a surprise for me. I don't know how appropriate her borderline flirting was but I sure as hell liked it. Either way it did motivate me to keep going and grind hard all week at this job.

Towards the end of the week I took a drive back to New Britain, a couple days later than I planned to originally. It felt like another world just driving there with all the traffic. I might as well have been transported to another galaxy. It turns out someone was assaulted and robbed right in our parking lot. So, what better time to finally leave? I let my cousin check up on the place. He was the one responsible cousin who didn't drink alcohol or do drugs, so I didn't have to worry about him trashing the place, having a bender, throwing a party. After my lease was up I'd be gone for good.

Chapter 5

This is not what I expected

I'd felt like a new man, prepared and ready to fly solo on my new job. I was officially on my own today, Monday. Up early to start at six a.m. I was surprised to see Cassandra downstairs at the desk at that early hour.

"You worked all night?" I asked.

"Yeah, our night auditor is on vacation. He gets back soon, in a few days."

I felt bad for her and started to put the pieces of the puzzle together. She'd been crying the other night because she works constantly and doesn't sleep enough. I don't know how much money she makes but I hope it's enough. In my case, I'm taking a pay cut, but I figure I'd stick it out and see how things go. Maybe I'd move up the ladder in this business or switch gears to something else later.

I got to work on my daily tasks. I kept calling Sandy over on the walkie talkie with questions. How was I supposed to know it all myself after one week of training? There were all these request codes in the computer and forty-five guests arriving today. Some of them wanted a pond view and I still didn't know off the top of my head which rooms constituted having a pond view. We had three floors all in one building and one elevator, which supposedly has malfunctioned numerous times last year, but is now operational. One hundred ten rooms total was a manageable number of rooms according to Ralph.

Sandy came over after I'd called her a couple times on the walkie talkie. She forcibly rested the broom in her hand up against the front desk counter making a smacking sound. She had a look of angry frustration on her face. "I'm sorry Sandy, I just want to know exactly which rooms are considered a pond view. Because I know that I don't see the pond from 219 for instance." She shuffled through some papers behind me and grabbed a laminated hotel map. She opened the drawer and took out a red Sharpie marker and wrote out my name on the hotel map. Then she slammed it down on the counter.

"You see these codes here next to each room? This represents which are pond view. That's your copy, you keep it. Any more questions?"

"Well, yeah actually when can I give someone until for a late check out? Because I'm seeing these requests in the system here and I just don't know what's acceptable?"

"Give one p.m., no later! OK?"

"Yes sure."

"Two housekeepers called out today and I'm cleaning rooms, and did I tell you the houseperson for the a.m. called out? We were supposed to hire back up for the overnight shift but that didn't happen either."

"I'm sorry Sandy." I could sense tears in her eyes and she was overwhelmed. I don't know what possessed me to say so, but I asked, "Is there anything more I can do? Like as far as picking up more shifts?" Ordinarily I'd be too cautious to ask about taking on that much work but damn, they were short staffed. I also realized pretty quickly that she was the only manager here which meant that I'd easily have an opportunity to progress to assistant general manager or something of the like if at all they'd create an opportunity for me.

"Brandon, look, let's sit down with this clipboard and pen. We went out into the center of the lobby where the free coffee station was located. "OK, look, work tonight till seven p.m. That's an extra four hours more than what you're scheduled plus you started early today, sorry." She started to perk up a little when she realized that I was going to be helping her big time. "I need to get some sleep before then. Next, come down tomorrow for six a.m. again. Head out of here at four? OK? Get some sleep if you can. Come back for eleven p.m., cover the overnight shift. I'll come to relieve you at seven a.m. OK?"

"No problem."

The day wore on and it went pretty well. I suppose it's all just a learning experience. Step by step I checked in guest after guest. Sandy was mopping floors, cleaning rooms and occasionally coming by to help me out. At one point we had ourselves a big high five moment. Our hands slapped in celebration of all our hard work accomplished. I figured I'd make the most of tonight considering I worked so hard and it was seven at night. I'd not have to work the graveyard shift until tomorrow night plus the night after. Following that night, the regular night auditor would be back from vacation, so I'd have the night off and presumably Sandy would also. Maybe I'd get a chance to actually have dinner with her. She'd continued to promise me that she had something special for me if I kept up all the hard work, so whatever it was, it kept me motivated. Perhaps it was a bonus check.

I drove out to that local sports bar. The Moose Pub. I called Sam; he wasn't available. Busy with the wife and kid. I felt a little intimidated to call Lex; the guy seemed a little too important to bother. He was like the big shot in town after all. I'd be curious to know more about his family. Siblings and so forth, where he lives. Frank was available, he'd meet me there. This was a nice bunch of people though, to exchange numbers with me and welcome me to town. Missy was there, just coincidently. Maybe she just liked to drink. I walked towards her, she had a friend with her whom she introduced as Sally. A blonde with rosy red, chubby cheeks and wearing a denim jacket and hoop earrings. I don't know what possessed me to do it, but I reached in and gave Missy a light hug and a kiss on each check. The truth is, I just plain find her attractive plus maybe subconsciously, her friend being there made me feel the urge to greet her that way. Her friend was cute also, but I didn't know her, so I didn't reach in to hug or kiss her, although I've done things like that in the past. It's funny in life, sometimes we do bold things and sometimes we don't. Frank and I ordered our second round of beers.

"What's your passion in life Brandon?" he asked.

"Well, ever since I was a teenager I totally changed my life by losing weight. You should've seen me. It had to have been close to seventy-five pounds I shed."

"What brings you to a little town in the sticks like this? We don't have a store like the one you worked for. Those clothes you won't find unless you get out to the mall or whatever. Tell me something more about yourself."

"I always had a gift for art you know? Like drawing, a little bit of painting but how much can I learn without studying? I suppose nowadays with YouTube and all, but still."

"I went to art school," Frank said in a matter of fact tone.

"Really?"

"Paier College of Art, two years then I transferred my credits over to the state school out here. You know, Eastern."

"You drove out there?"

"Haddam. Yeah, not too far from here."

"Actually, it's Hamden," I responded.

"Yeah," he said.

"I had a catalog from their school back in the late 90s. I still have it actually. But instead of art school, I took courses a little over a year at CCSU then dropped out," I explained to Frank.

I felt I caught him in a lie. I was suspicious of Frank from the beginning. He just seemed like a somewhat dangerous character, but I let it go as I was in uncharted territory out here. Hell, I never even knew this town a week ago and now it's home. The question is: How could he have attended a college for two years and think it was in Haddam when in reality it's in Hamden? There's no way. Those two towns are at least forty-five minutes to an hour apart.

"I got to take a piss," he said.

On his way to the bathroom he accidently bumped into a man, much bigger than him. Frank was a short guy but not an ounce of fat on him. "Mother fucker," he mumbled as the man passed. Definitely he was a tough character. By my age, mid-thirties, I've at least learned to not be so naïve. Many people out there are going to tell lies.

I walked over to Missy and her blonde friend Sally. "Hi ladies," I said. Missy raised her glass of beer and tapped it to mine. Sally giggled then picked up her glass and did the same. "Salud!"

"So, have both of you always lived out here in Pine Creek?" I asked.

"Yeah," they both said simultaneously, laughing afterwards. "Well, Sally went to Eastern Connecticut State University, so she commuted, and I went to Salve Regina in Newport, so I got away from this podunk town for a few years. Then moved outside Providence. Got engaged. Broke up. Moved back here," Missy said.

"So, you both graduated from Pine Creek High?" I asked.

"What? There's actually no Pine Creek High," Missy responded.

"Where'd you get an idea like that Brandon?!" Sally joked while she slapped me on the shoulder."

"Frank said he graduated from there. Class of 2001."

"Franks a loser," Missy said while Sally laughed a little.

"You're telling me that there is no such school?" I asked.

"Correct," Sally responded.

"He attended Paier College of Art for a couple years?" I asked.

"Where?"

"He's not an artist at all?" I asked.

"Frank is a wannabe thug," Missy said.

"Don't tell him we said that, Sally added. "He works for Lex sometimes and we don't know what he's capable of," Sally added.

"Like a mafia type of thing?" I asked.

"Shhh he's coming now," Sally said. Missy looked around the room trying to erase the conversation we just had and replace it with something entirely different.

"Let's have a smoke Brandon," Frank said.

"OK." I walked out the front of the Moose Pub with him as he handed me a cig. He reached over to light it up for me as I took in a drag. I didn't want to say anything, but this was the first smoke I'd had in probably five years. Oh well. I was never really a smoker anyways. Just casually.

"You see those women there getting out that black Honda?" he asked.

"Yeah, sure, the curvy tall lady and then the thinner one with her hair back?"

"Yeah, I know them. I can introduce you sometime," Frank said.

"Sure, how about now?"

We came back inside, and all of us stood around drinking our beers and cocktails. The two ladies came over to Frank and he introduced me to them. One of them gave me a seductive look and I began to wonder if the benefits to hanging around Frank were worth the risks.

"Oh God, it's getting late." I lifted my left arm and glanced at my watch. "I've got to get going buddy," I said.

I headed back to catch enough sleep to be up early to work the next day.

Day in and day out I worked and worked at that hotel. I had some rest in between and some days I just worked myself to the bone. It was a "sink or swim" experience with no real training on the graveyard shift with the exception of Sandy working with me for one hour. That night she was yawning repeatedly and even fell asleep suddenly, her head hitting the table causing a clunking sound. She'd excused herself at that point and said I'd be okay on my own for the rest of the night. Finally, Thursday was approaching and all I had to do was work until eleven p.m., then I'd be a free man, able to sleep through the night. Coincidentally this was the night Sandy said she'd have her surprise for me.

Chapter 6

The surprise I was waiting for

I'd trudged up to my room, finally, after 11:15 p.m. Hey, at least I didn't have to drive home after work. All I needed now was a good stereo in this room, so I could play some of my CDs. I had my laptop with me, so I spent a lot of my free time surfing the web, looking at social media and flipping through channels on the TV. The Weather Channel, 24-hour news networks, true crime shows, etc. I jumped in the shower and rinsed off. I felt refreshed after putting on a white tee shirt and pajama bottoms. I checked to make sure the temperature on the AC was cool enough. Indeed, it was refreshingly cold. I laid back on my bed and felt my neck relax as it rested on top of the foam pillow. Where's that surprise after all? I guess she was full of it. What was she doing, just motivating me to keep working like an idiot all week long? I *did* learn a lot of stuff. I'd say it's true I have a positive attitude in life, always trying to find the positive in a negative situation. I had saved up enough money as a safety net from my last career plus now I can take these new skills and use them elsewhere if I had to. After all, there's got to be hotels less dysfunctional than this one, right?

Knock, knock, knock, knock…. I heard someone at my door. I reluctantly sat up out of bed and opened the door. It was Sandy. "Hi, I have the night off," she said.

I walked back towards the bed. "Come in."

"You can take a seat back on the bed, I know you're tired, you worked all week so hard," she said. I sat back down on the bed, but this time leaned my back up against the headboard. She had the same navy-blue dress on which I saw her in the first day along with the pearl necklace and brown shoes. She laid her purse down on the desk. Then she picked up my bottle of water off the desk and quenched her thirst. I thought that was a kind of personal thing to do but peculiarly sexy, nonetheless. Next, she lifted her left leg, bending it across her right leg and pulled off her shoe, then she did the same with her right shoe, gently removing it. Neatly, she placed both shoes side by side by the desk. "Do you mind if I take this off?" While she asked me, she began to remove her dress before I could respond. There she was standing across the room from me in her bra and panties. Next her necklace came off. My eyes were fixated on her. I actually tried not to blink. Cassandra walked slowly across the room towards me. She got on top of me and began kissing my lips. Now, whether this was appropriate or not based on employee relations was one thing, but I didn't have any strength to resist the temptation. Here was an opportunity literally knocking on my door. So, this was the surprise she promised me. We had sex that night. What a week it's been.

Part Two

Chapter 7

The pace of life

One day flowed into the next while my paychecks flowed towards me. I made my way around town to explore more than just what Lex and his family owned. The bank, where I deposited my checks which included all the crazy overtime hours I'd put in, the local park, the post office where I sent out a few postcards to my niece and nephew, and even the consignment store where I picked up a used true crime book from a case in 1998, the remains of a car burned down on the cover, palm trees in the distance and a firetruck and police cruiser on the scene…looked interesting. Also, a used coffee mug which read: "LIFE IS A GRIND!" It was illustrated with a steaming mug and coffee beans piled up and scattered about. I liked the teal, yellow and pink colors. It had an 80s motif to it. All these years I tend to cling to things from that era. What can I say? It inspires me.

Back at the hotel I developed a solid work ethic from all the hours I'd put in. Several weeks had gone by since I'd first started there and more or less I'd developed a certain level of competence. Still there was a part of me that felt I'd have to work at a hotel for a solid year full-time in order to *really* get the hang of it.

I could see Cassandra out of the corner of my eyes walking towards me as I stood behind the long desk. I found Cassandra to be a sexier name as compared to Sandy, so I sort of toggled back and forth between the two. She stopped behind me and put her right hand on my right shoulder and her left hand on my left shoulder. It felt really good. But this wasn't the first time she'd done it since a few weeks ago when we slept together. It was a regular occurrence which only got me wondering about the cameras rolling. Considering Lex and his father owned the hotel, they had access to all the footage and so forth. Personally, I didn't really care much. I simply was going along for the ride. She leaned her face in close to mine and whispered in my right ear. "You're a very sexy man Brandon." I got chills up and down my body.

We continued to sleep together as the days went by. Some weeks it was twice and other weeks we did it three or four times per week. One time we passed the corner of the first floor and checked to see if the coast was clear. We then proceeded to make out passionately for at least two minutes. Plain and simple, it was a heated romance which I thrived on.

Our regular night auditor had been back for weeks now, so I didn't have to fill in on the overnight shift during the week, yet I did have to fill in occasionally on a Friday or Saturday night since he had those nights off. Cassandra also filled in with the occasional part-timer pulling an all-nighter for us albeit reluctantly. Can you blame them? Maxine has little kids at home and Ralph was an older guy. He probably was around retirement age but then again, I didn't really want to ask his age. And then there was the night auditor. Somehow, I felt like he was avoiding me in conversation because I'd not gotten the chance to talk with him beyond the necessary pass-on notes in the log book we related to each other at the exchanging of shifts.

I finally had a day off, thus I decided to head back to the park. I jogged for one hour taking walking breaks in between. To my amazement, the water fountain actually worked and I sure as hell needed it. The temperature reached 92 degrees.

Later I spent some time next door to the hotel at the "shopping center" which Lex's family owned. First, I stopped at the Starlight for a bite to eat. I had a large salad with croutons, black beans, chickpeas, cucumbers, green peppers, but held the tomatoes and onions. Being a vegetarian is not always easy, but I find it exciting after all these years nonetheless. You've got to be resourceful.

Next, I walked through the indoor section of the shopping center. I am one who could stop to appreciate the little details like the shape of the massive window to my left and the bench in the center of the hallway where you could sit and face any direction. I suppose the bench was in the shape of an octagon. I didn't take the time to count the sides of it. I just kept walking towards the coffee shop on the right. London Fog Café the sign read. I wonder if they had an actual connection to London, England? Lex's family and all. Regardless I loved coffee shops, so I approached it. Before I got the chance to step in, I saw Frank. He waved his hand in the air and said, "See you tonight! Gotta head in the auto part store. Damn blinker's broken."

I wondered what he was talking about when he mentioned *seeing me tonight*. I didn't give it much more thought but welcomed the friendliness this town/village had to offer. I got myself a massive black and white cookie with a large mug of house blend coffee, unsweetened with milk. I sat there and took bites of it leisurely since I had time to myself. The smell of the cookie and sweet taste in my mouth lingered. I ripped off a chunk of the soft cookie and dipped it into my mug. Soft rock music played on the radio while I glanced around the café. It was that 80s song *Sara* from the band *Starship*. Indeed, the room was really shaped quite like a triangle which was different. A small place but enough room for several to congregate in. At this specific time, it was empty with the exception of myself and the girl behind the counter.

Chapter 8

Trouble is brewing

After my decadent black and white cookie with coffee, I leisurely walked next door to my hotel room. Halfway there I panicked for a moment realizing my cellphone was not in my pocket. *Must be in my hotel room*, I thought. Couldn't be in my car. I seldomly drove anywhere anymore since I lived right where I worked and had the shopping center all in the same spot.

I bolted up the stairs to my room on the second level. I still never tried the elevator. Maybe subconsciously I was afraid it would malfunction. I heard staff joking about how it was out of service on and off last year. Nah, I was just looking for ways to keep my metabolism up. When it comes to dealing with hotel guests though, they had a policy: what they don't know can't hurt them! I didn't like the dishonesty but Harry, the night auditor told me that dishonesty and the hotel business go together like peanut butter and jelly. Yet when he said it he sounded pissed. Maybe he was an honest guy like me.

I checked my cellphone. It was there on the nightstand. No messages. I suppose I should get a quick workout in downstairs. I'm off work all day and all night. What the hell else am I going to do? So, I did a bit of circuit training using the free weights covering all the major muscle groups. I drank more water today than usual. It must have been the oppressive heat or my earlier jog outdoors that did it.

I took a long cool shower and laid out on the bed. I felt more relaxed than ever. After a couple minutes I got up and made myself an evening coffee using the free stuff in the room. I used my coffee mug from the consignment store which read "LIFE IS A GRIND!" Next, I booted up my laptop and signed into Facebook. It felt good to hear the gentle sound of the air conditioning while I felt the cold air blowing along my bare legs and arms. What was everybody up to? I didn't forget about my staff at the clothing store. Karen was always posting stuff. I stopped to like some of her funny memes and pics of her. Cassandra of all people here at the hotel would not connect with anyone because of the manager/employee relationship. Funny for obvious reasons. Jane was still in my thoughts somewhere back there in the recesses of my mind. I still remember her face and her tears as she said goodbye to me. Yet nothing posted on Facebook with the exception of her new position in Rhinebeck, New York. A medium sized town on the Hudson where they'd built a new store especially bigger than ours in Avon. She'd head it as general manager. Congratulations to her but I hope she still is single if I ever see her again.

I turned on the TV and came across a network playing movies. It was a thriller from the past starring Michael Douglas. I was fond of how he was a natural on screen without having to try hard. I think a certain kind of intelligence was easily portrayed by his overall appearance and mannerisms. Forget about his comedic or romantic abilities; it's how he portrayed pure anger when he had to that moved me. It actually gave me goose bumps. I got into the movie and forgot about my laptop. After several minutes I felt the urge to shut off the TV and head into town for a drink at the Moose Pub. Maybe it was the coffee which gave me a jolt or maybe it was the Jack Daniels and Coke I saw being served in a bar scene in the movie. Regardless I had the night off so why not?

I got in my car and headed across town. Although it seems odd to some, smooth jazz music was one of my great inspirations in life which helped me to lose that seventy-five pounds I spoke of earlier. So, I slid in a CD by Richard Elliott. I'd seen him play a live show back in New Haven a couple years ago and found his work impressive. The song playing in my car was called *Mystery*. I adjusted the AC so that I could breathe in some fresh cool air. Arriving at the Moose I stumbled upon Sam. OK, so I wouldn't just be a loner tonight out at the bar. We were talking about life and all when I noticed he'd always glance over my shoulder in the distance.

"Is everything OK?"

"Yeah, It's just Frank. I know he's out there. He kept coming back in and out tonight. He asked about you too." Sam said.

Sam was actually a doctor. A pharmacist to be exact. He'd worked at the Pine Creek Village Pharmacy next to the London Fog Café I'd visited earlier. Growing up in Pine Creek, he was the regular guy in town. Everyone loved him, and he'd basically been best friends with Lex forever. Lex's little sister had a crush on Sam for years; now she's nineteen. A complete knockout. Tall, skinny, long blonde hair and she's even modeling. Professionally. Sam was now not only married but had a little one at home also. He'd been involved with local government and even attended Ivy League college to study pharmacy in New York City. Columbia. That's where he met his wife.

"My wife, she fell in love with Pine Creek Village, this tiny shit town Brandon. She's from the city, New York. Grew up right there. Went to Columbia with me. I was president of my fraternity. We dated. Things got serious. I took her to visit my family out here in Pine Creek. She fell in love with it. I repeat. She actually fell in love with this place. That's why we're here. I still have the urge to move south. Palm trees, beaches. Just think…no more bone chilling Connecticut winters. Maybe the wife will come around to this idea one day."

"But Sam, what about Frank? You said he'd been asking about me?"

"Forget about Frank. He's going nowhere in life. You're better off staying away from him but don't let anyone know I told you that," Sam said, in a scolding manner while he shook his index finger at me.

I looked puzzled but continued my conversation with Sam. "I think your wife just got tired of living in New York City all those years, plus she took one look at your family and realized you guys were a solid New England family with ties to all the right people in town. A good place to raise kids, right? Its natural out here, no? Ideal."

"Yeah, I hear you," Sam responded then took a long swig of beer out of his pint glass.

I had ordered one while we were chatting and got about halfway through my ale. "You guys are rich, no wonder," I said. The alcohol was affecting me quickly.

"What do you mean?" he snapped back.

"I mean, your wife took a look at your family's house. All the acres, the luxury of it all and presto," I responded.

"You googled it right? Where I live?"

"I was curious about Lex. He runs this town, right? Naturally I was curious about where you lived also or where your family was from. What this place is all about."

"Well I don't blame you. Just don't waste your time at that hotel for too long. You can do better."

"Come on let's go." Sam led the way outside the bar in a stealthy manner like as if we were The Hardy Boys. "Shhhh…follow me."

We stepped outside, and he put out his left arm to block me from moving forward. Then looked at me seriously and continued to walk forward. "Come on," he whispered.

I suppose he wanted me to follow him, so I walked carefully behind him then heard a screeching sound like fingernails on a chalkboard. Looking ahead to my amazement I saw Frank keying a car. His hand tightly griping a set of keys with his right elbow bent, he firmly scraped across the back of the vehicle. I turned and looked the other way. Sam looked right at me then grabbed my lapel and we walked inside the bar.

"Just avoid him, don't think about it. It's not your car," he said.

"Are you crazy? But shouldn't we do something?" I asked.

"Frank works for Lex. For all we know he could have had Frank do that," Sam said.

"But he was asking about me??" I said while feeling worried.

"Yeah, he was, wasn't he?"

"You're scared of Frank, right? So, you don't want to stir the pot," I asked.

Sam stood there without responding.

"I get it. Frank works for Lex. You're friends with Lex."

"This is my life Brandon. I'm a fairly well-paid pharmacist whose job is in the hands of Lex and Lex's dad basically. If Franky wants to go do his mafia shit, let it be."

"Do you think that he was going for my car? He got mixed up maybe?" I asked.

Sam's phone went off. It was a text message from his wife. "Listen Brandon. Let's finish up this beer and have another one on another night.

Better yet let's talk at the park tomorrow. Six p.m.? Ok with you?"

"Yeah, at six. Looking forward to it Doc!"

Chapter 9

Getting the inside scoop

I went back to my hotel room, yet I only drank one pint of beer at the Moose, so I checked my fridge to see if I had anymore. Four more beers were left, ice cold, so I figured I'd at least crack another one and see what else was on that movie network. The Michael Douglas film was over by now, but another action flick was playing. Christian Slater and Minnie Driver were on screen in the film *Hard Rain*. I actually never saw this one yet somehow knew I'd like it on in the background while I sipped my beer. At the least, the sound of the heavy rain in the film might help me sleep. A close up shot of Minnie Driver appeared on the TV. I fixed my gaze on her. That thick dark curly hair did something for me. *Damn she was cute,* I thought.

I found myself puzzled over Frank. What did he mean earlier in the day when he said he'd see me tonight? Why did he ask Sam about my whereabouts, repeatedly?

I fell asleep soundly but later woke up concerned about my life. Would Frank key my car tomorrow? Or would he beat me up? With a weapon? What about Lex?

I happened to be up earlier than my alarm was set to go off. No sense in getting back to bed now. Shave, shower, brush my teeth, floss, get dressed, splash on some cologne and I'd be ready to rumble. I casually trotted down the stairs and around the corner passing the front desk. I lifted my right arm in the air and said good morning to Harry who'd been working the overnight shift. After clocking in I poured scolding hot water over my oatmeal in a medium sized ceramic bowl. Raisins, walnuts, maple syrup. Good enough. I'll let that cool off while I walk over to relieve hard working Harry. Anyone who'd been up all night plus had the regular unenviable position of full time status on the graveyard shift deserved to be labeled as "hard working." On second thought, generally the graveyard shift had a lot less customers so who was really the hard working one?

"Shoot! I forgot to get coffee. Do you mind Harry?"

"No, go for it."

I ran over to the coffee station and poured myself a cup then walked behind the long desk and sipped my java. "What do you got for me?" I asked.

"OK, well here are the pass-ons." Harry picked up the "Red book" and flipped open to last night's entry. "Room 110 is having issues with their toilet. Have the engineer check on it anytime after eight a.m. He'll be out at business meetings all day after then. Room's 157 and 158 are going to need two p.m. late check outs. I approved it so just let it be! We're slow so we can have an easy turn around today."

I was listening to him while rubbing my chin with my right hand. I thought about asking him more about himself and whether or not he liked his job here. *Did the guy not like me?* I wondered.

"So what kind of music do you like Harry?"

"I used to love the Dave Matthews Band, but I got sick of them. I can't believe I'm even saying so after being obsessed with their music for so long. Who would have thought they'd kick the violinist out of the band or whatever happened there or that the sax player would die? That's not the Dave Matthews Band I loved back in the day. I mean, the more I think about it.... without Leroi....the style of music is not the same. Boyd, well, I don't know what to say."

I actually broke the ice there. For the first time Harry opened up to me a bit and spoke about something other than the contents of the pass-on log. "I think Dave and company need to change their direction myself. Although not many would agree with me, but I think they could have a jazzier sound. Like even smooth jazz or instrumental," I remarked.

"You hit the hammer on the head, Brandon. It's like they're trying too hard to appeal to a certain fan base, the critics-although they'd never admit that- or just some type of definition of authentic music, but it's not working for me. Is it *them* trying to appeal to that fan base and all that stuff though or is it mostly Dave himself? I don't know," he responded.

"I was dying, when you were gone. You know, back when you were on vacation. I covered shifts like a mother fucker," I whispered the last couple words. It was quiet in the lobby and not much excitement at all at this hour especially.

"I've worked in hotels for over eleven fucking years. You know, it's good to hear what you said about the struggle to work all those shifts man, because we gotta express how we feel sometimes. Back when I was at a chain hotel, before this place, everyone was pretty much just faking their way through the day. You know? 'I love my job…blah blah blah' b-u-l-l shit! But coming here out to the sticks was refreshing. I was almost not gonna do it either. I just figured I had the experience in hotels, so I came here. The difference is worth pointing out-between corporate run hotels and family run."

It was good to hear him finally vent a little. And hey, I'm no sucker, I've been through ten years at the clothing store. I've seen that business. Been there done that. Now I want the inside scoop here from Harry's point of view. "Is it true they call you 'Tips and tricks Harry?" I was a little nervous to point that out as I didn't want to piss him off. I suppose Harry had a protective shell around him that made him come across I don't know….

"Yeah, that's cool."

"Because you know the system so well. The night audit and all the commands in the computer. You've trained so many people." I paused for a moment then continued speaking. "You're 'tips and tricks Harry' because everyone goes to you with questions on how to do stuff."

"Thanks. Cassandra knows her stuff too. I give her credit on that. She's GM after all, I don't have what it takes to go that route. I do in a way but also, I don't because I don't have that personality. Strengths and weaknesses Brandon, strengths and weaknesses, that's what I say. We're not all going to be good at the same thing. Like you were saying before, 'I know the system so well' but I hate the system! It's like this guy who worked here as houseperson with me on nights before he quit. He had two jobs, so I don't know how he managed but he'd say, 'Everyone hates America but they all come to America.' He was a foreign guy here in America for I don't know how many years, but you know what he means? People criticize America all over the world but if their country is poor they come here anyways for the opportunity. He was laughing when he said it, so it was actually kind of funny. You've got to have a sense of humor. But you know what's hard Brandon?" Harry asked me.

"No, what?"

"This guy Chip, who worked here on the night shift before me, odd guy. Yeah, I know I'm a little odd myself but anyways he'd answered the phone and dealt with a guest complaint. He made a joke and then he turned to me and said 'humor, you've got to have a sense of humor to lighten things up.' So, he means that you're making the situation better for the guest and just overall. *But* I can't do that much. I can joke with the coworkers but with the guests? You're taking a risk. What if they get even madder after you incorporate humor?"

"You've got a point Harry. You mentioned Cassandra. Is she kinda touchy feely with you at all? Just something I noticed about her," I asked him somewhat hesitatingly.

"Yeah, yeah…this one time she came from behind me when I was just looking online. I was bored pissless Brandon. It was perfect timing because I was about to lose my mind from boredom. She'd started rubbing my shoulders and then she went to my neck."

"Sooo, what'd you do?" I asked.

"I said to her, 'that's nice'," Harry responded.

"Then…then what?" I asked. In truth I was curious to know how far Cassandra went with her other employees. I'd developed feelings for her obviously and needed to know what kind of person she really was.

"She stopped for a second or two then she reached for the back of my head and touched my hair. It was nice, but I couldn't reciprocate anything further with her because she's my boss," Harry said.

"I don't blame you Harry."

"What about you?"

"She does the same thing to me," I told him.

"And how far did she take it with you?"

He looked in my eyes. I hesitated, not knowing what to say. I was too honest to lie. "I *want* her Harry, she's a sexy lady," I said.

"She's been with Lex," Harry said in a quieter tone of voice.

This got me upset but I didn't know what to say. It caused me to have that feeling. You know that feeling that just rushes through your body and isn't pleasant.

I think Harry knew there was something between Cassandra and I, so he just kept talking about her as a way to get all his thoughts and feelings out about her. "I'll tell you this, she's sneaky as hell. Keep an eye on your phone," Harry said.

"Why?" I asked.

"Dude, I better clock out now. We've been chatting for over half an hour. I don't want to get in trouble for milking the clock," he said as he picked up his bag and coffee tumbler heading out.

The day continued rather typically. More or less uneventfully yet I wondered about Franky and I wondered about Lex screwing Cassandra. I wondered about what Harry didn't finish telling me about 'watching my phone'. What the hell did he mean by that? Connecting it to Cassandra too. Before that he said she's sneaky.

94

I started googling more about Pine Creek Village. I already knew Frank was lying about attending the high school as it didn't exist. He'd also lied about the population. According to Wikipedia the town was smaller than the smallest towns in Connecticut such as Beacon Falls. It was actually really tiny but officially had its own zip code and was an independent town yet previously a part of a larger town historically speaking. I learned a lot from the internet, but I also learned a lot from Harry, indeed he earned his nickname "tips and tricks." I looked forward to after work, so I could meet up with Sam in the park. There I'd continue to learn about this paradoxical little town some more.

Chapter 10

Do I belong here?

Bright, warm and pleasant at six p.m. That's something I loved about summertime. I met up with Sam near the parking spaces closest to the basketball courts in the park. We walked and conversed while passing by the pool. We heard splashing and laughing and talking. Some people were laid out on a towel on the grass sunbathing.

"I used to come here with the wife swimming before we had a kid. It was nice. Pretty soon we'll be coming back when the kid's old enough to want to swim," Sam said taking a gulp from his Poland Spring water bottle.

"Is it true Sam, that Lex was together with Cassandra?"

"I don't know about *together*."

"Sam, can you tell me the real honest truth about this situation?"

"Listen Brandon. Don't say A-N-Y-T-H-I-N-G, OK? Here's the thing, I'm buddy-buddy with Lex; you *know* that. He's been my best friend all my life.

"Yeah."

"He's kept it from *me* even. But I'm a smart cookie. I've spent God knows how many hours at Lex's mansion or his guest house where he lives," Sam said, his eyebrows furrowed.

"Yes, and...and?" I responded.

He glanced around and spoke in his characteristic serious and quieter tone. "I saw a framed photo of Cassandra in Lex's guest house. In the bedroom. Under a stack of things. I was nosey. Lex had gotten up to replenish our drinks but by the time he'd be back I'd have enough time to snoop around the place since he'd have to go to the main house for a bottle of vodka, have a smoke, use the bathroom."

"Framed photo of Cassandra huh?"

"Then I slip the photo out of the frame. Turn it around. Written in red ink: Love you Lexy! You sexy guy! Sandy. With of course a heart drawn plus some kissy lips," Sam explained.

"Oh God, the plot thickens. OK well at least now I know. I mean technically I don't know everything but I'm no kid anymore. I've been through heartbreak and I'm no fool. I know anyone willing to get in my bed with me like the way she did was just that type of woman," I explained.

"What?!" So, *you* did it with Cassandra *as well*?"

"Ohhh shoot, OK I didn't mean to talk about that but yeah," I said.

We walked and talked throughout the park. "You want to grab a couple rounds at the Moose, Brandon?"

"Your wife's not going to mind?" I asked.

"I'll tell her I'm with you. Women like you around here Brandon. But don't let it go to your head!" he joked.

Sam followed me to the hotel and left his car in the far back corner of the parking lot. We ordered a taxi to be responsible. He'd said he didn't care if he got smashed, he'd just make sure he didn't get behind the wheel. 'I deserve a good couple few drinks don't I Brandon?' he'd said.

We were having a blast at the bar and I somehow felt comforted by the fact that Sam was a friend who seemed to have my back. I was still concerned with Franky and I wondered about Cassandra. I lost interest in wanting any serious relationship with her, but I still felt like I had to ask so called "Harry tips and tricks" what he meant about her *messing with people's phones.*

Suddenly the two women I'd remembered from a while back strolled in the bar. They were the ones Franky wanted to introduce me to. One who was rather voluptuous and heavy set, the other especially skinny with her hair tied back. Whatever it was they both came across seductive looking. No lie, I was attracted by them both. "We were supposed to be having fun the other night Brandon. *Where were you?*" one of them said.

"Really?" I was excited and surprised at the same time. What were they talking about?

"We were going to have some fun. You, Me, her, and Franky," she said it all kind of slowly, so I could catch on to what was happening.

"And yooouuu," she began to say as she slid her hand across Sam's upper back, "are off limits now that you're married."

Sam looked visibly uncomfortable. I studied him for a second and could see sweat forming on his face. He took a deep breath.

"Let's take a shot guys," Sam offered. "It's on me! Southern Comfort OK?"

"We've got to run boys. Frank told us not to get involved with you Brandon, after the other night when you stood us up."

"Don't say that," one of the ladies responded as she lightly slapped her friend on the shoulder. "Byeee," she accentuated the word.

What am I, back in college here? What is going on in this town? It's like some kind of soap opera out here, I thought to myself.

"Follow me Brandon," Sam walked over to the bartender and ordered us a couple Southern Comforts and a round of beers. In truth we were feeling buzzed pretty quickly tonight we both noticed. Must have been something in the air, but it felt good as usual. I don't know what's gotten into me tonight, but I pressed Sam about the ladies.

"That chick was awfully friendly with you there Sam. Like when she slid her hand over your back," I mentioned.

"Yeah, I fooled around with her. The skinny one. Before I was married. My girlfriend was still on her final year at Columbia and I was out here and there. Working internships, visiting back home. Frank hooked me up with her and it's all in the past. If you say anything I'll kill you! OK?!" Sam said, his eyes bulging out.

"Yeah sure." I didn't have any further response for Sam. I was shocked at what degenerate behavior he'd been up to. Cheating on his girlfriend, now wife like that. But at the same time, I realized he'd been a frat boy which typically isn't synonymous with morality.

It was getting late and we decided to head back. We were both feeling drunk and when we got to the hotel parking lot I asked Sam to stop in the lobby to say hello to Harry. After all, it was past eleven p.m. so he was on the clock. The lobby was completely dead at that point.

"You guys are drunk. That's what I like to see," Harry said with a chuckle. We rested up against the counter and shot the breeze for a while with Harry.

"Can I buy a beer?" Sam asked then walked over to the fridge in the lobby and picked out a Coors Light, twisted off the cap and took a swig then hiccupped.

Because I was a bit inebriated I spoke more freely to Harry. "Harry, why didn't you talk to me more before this morning? You're very guarded it seems. Your too damn serious. You need to lighten up."

"You know what Brandon. I am not really easy around people all the time. Why do you think I work the night audit? It's less people and more printing reports. Who do you think stocks up all those snacks and stuff in our shop there? Who do you think…"

"You're getting off topic Harry."

"OK listen, you came in here like this pretty boy who worked at that clothing store. I had female guests in this damn hotel asking about you! I guess I was just a little intimidated by you. It's my personality," Harry said.

"OK I hear you Harry. What were you saying about Cassandra before and watching out for your phones?"

"OK yeah, but you didn't hear it from me." He put his hand on the counter. I caught her looking at my phone before. Flipping through all my personal stuff, whatever. And she saw me catch her in the act too," Harry said.

"Wait a minute, stop right there, guys," Sam said pointing his index finger up in the air. His speech was slightly slurred. "Listen guys, listen…OK I've got a theory. Cassandra is nosey, she's twisted. She's snooping on Harry's phone. She's working non-stop hours. She's a mother fuckin workaholic, so am I, but that's beside the point, she's got issues. She's messing with Brandon's phone which explains why you didn't have your phone the other day with you and you found it by your nightstand that day. Is it a coincidence that you didn't have any messages in your phone from Frank even though he was looking for you that night? And not just looking for you, he kept looking for you and asking about you."

"H-o-l-y shit! He walked past me in the shopping center that day saying he'd see me tonight. So, then Cassandra goes in my hotel room. She obviously has access to get in there. She deletes the messages from Frank and therefore I never know to meet Frank at the Moose Pub that night. Instead I go there and see Sam then have a round with him. Frank is outside keying a car, pissed off, then leaves. Sam you're a genius. You're a doctor after all," I say.

"But why would Cassandra delete Brandon's messages from Frank?" Harry asks.

"Those two seductive ladies at the Moose Pub, Sam begins to say. They were going to have a wild night of sex with our friend Brandon here. And Cassandra's no dummy. She knew that. Everybody who hangs around Franky ends up hooking up with ladies. He makes that happen for people. So, Cassandra wants

Brandon having no part of that," Sam explains and then takes a long swig of his bottled beer.

"Give me that! I reach for his beer half joking."

"Get your own damn beer!" Sam responds, still slurring his speech.

"OK doctor's orders." I head over to the fridge and grab a Heineken.

Harry grabs the beer from my hand and pops it open with a bottle opener he finds in the drawer behind the desk. "Church key," he says with a smile. "That's what they call these things in some places."

"Maybe out in the bible belt," Sam says then finishes off his brew, later reaching over in the fridge for another. "Put them all on my debit card Harry, thank you."

"Cassandra wants Brandon having no part of that? Harry repeats what Sam said just a minute ago. "She doesn't want Brandon out fooling around with Franky's female companions...hhhmmm? Why?"

"Because Cassandra wants him all to herself, elementary my dear Watson," Sam responds to Harry.

"Watch it," I say to Sam quietly as I push my finger into his chest.

Harry looks at me without saying a word. Sam is quiet for a moment. I'm also quiet as a mouse.

"OK, OK, Cassandra likes me and she's doing that whole touchy-feely thing you know how we talked about earlier Harry," I say.

Harry scrunches his eyebrows and looks at me more quizzically. "What's really going on between you and Cassandra Brandon?"

"OK you know what? She's fucking my brains out! And I like it, I like it a lot. We have a lot of fun, but you know what else?"

"What?" Harry asks.

"I've had just about enough of this place. This little town. And I'm not the only one with Cassandra. What about…." Sam stops me by putting his hand on my shoulder and giving me a look, which says not to say anything.

I regain my senses and realize that it would not be in my best interest to reveal that Cassandra has also slept with Lex in the past. I don't know what Harry is capable of saying or doing to make more trouble for me than I already have. So, we call it a night and say bye to Harry the night auditor.

Sam crashes on the sofa bed in my room and drives home in the morning. I suppose he'll have some explaining to do to his wife at that point.

Part Three

Chapter 11

Harry visits the flea market

Harry was pleased to be on his weekend break from work. Thursday night he was up all-night working at the hotel as always until Friday morning 7 a.m. and then he was a free man. Of course, the trouble was deciding whether to force himself to sleep Friday morning or to just stay up nearly twenty-four hours and comfortably crash Friday night. Decisions, decisions. Life wasn't getting any easier after all these years on the graveyard shift, but he'd made the most of it. He decided to crash early Friday evening and Saturday was up at an ungodly hour while most of America slept. With little to do as it was still pitch dark outside, he searched social media for events taking place. Harry decided upon a mostly indoor flea market and got there precisely when it opened.

A seedy looking place but worth exploring for someone who loved this sort of thing. Harry parked amidst a lot of broken-down cars left to rot, rusted pipes, and old broken wooden furniture. Was it the front entrance or the back entrance? It was a door anyways. Harry got out of his car and as he made his way to the door he saw three men talking and he walked toward them, then stopped for some reason to listen to their conversation. While they were talking, one of them pointed downward and said, "You dropped something. Looks like a coin."

The man, a very hefty fellow, then responded "Thanks," and reached down to pick up the coin off the ground while a loud enough to notice tearing sound followed. He'd ripped his pants along the backside exposing his boxer shorts through his khakis. The two men started chuckling which soon became uncontrollable laughter. Hysterical laughter. Harry joined in by laughing as he found it irresistible even though it was wrong he felt, to laugh at this mishap. Much like a yawn, the laughter was contagious.

The man who'd ripped his pants walked away and through the entrance of the flea market. "How could you guys laugh like that?" Harry asked with a serious expression on his face.

"What? You're laughing also. You shouldn't talk."

"Yeah," the other man said.

"I just feel bad for the guy, alright," Harry said as he walked away from the men and into the flea market.

Harry canvased the area looking around to see where the fat guy with the ripped pants had gone. "Ah ha," he said while spotting him looking methodically at a box filled with some type of DVD's. He picked one up, put it down, picked it up, then put it down again. Once again, he picked it up and examined it, turning it on an angle then put it back in the box. Using his index finger, he swept a line of dust off the DVD cases. I decided to walk up to him and say something.

"You know that movie up there?" Harry asked the heavy-set man while pointing up to a giant poster on the wall.

"No, but I recognize the guy. It's Steve

Guttenberg. He's from those *Police Academy* movies and the *Cocoon* films."

"Yeah but this one is 'The Bedroom Window,' 1987. What's interesting is that I believe it was his first serious thriller type of film. A departure from comedy. And I love thrillers. And of course, I love the 80s. Plus, he's very much like himself in the movie the way you'd expect him to be in a comedy.

"How do you mean?"

"Well, he's not angry, he's not even too serious. It's like he just gets caught up in this situation that gets really dangerous," Harry explained.

"So, don't spoil it for me or anything. I want to see it now."

"I'm Harry by the way."

"Guy."

"What guy?"

"No, I'm Guy. That's my name. G-U-Y. Guy."

"Oh OK, sorry."

"Oh no, don't worry about it. Happens all the time."

"You know something? I like the name Guy. It's a cool name. Who was that character from that arcade game?" Harry asked.

"Yeah, his name was Guy, Final Fight. The side scroller, beat up everyone in your path video game. That's what you're talking about? You had the mayor of the city, Haggar, real buff guy who wore the suspenders and did the wrestling moves and the boxer Cody, and then there was Guy, the martial artist," Guy explained.

"So, I'm assuming you're an 80s baby like me?" Harry asked.

"Yeah, we have that in common," Guy responded.

"I have the DVD of that movie you know?" Harry said while again pointing up at the giant poster.

"The Bedroom Window? I'd like to see it," Guy said.

"You want to watch it sometime?"

Guy and Harry fast became friends. In truth Harry felt bad for Guy's mishap with the torn pants while also realizing he'd wanted to make new friends himself and here was an opportunity. After all these years subjected to working the graveyard shift, his list of friends had dwindled down very low. It was clear to Harry also that Guy was dealing with a serious case of O.C.D. It's a little sad to see someone who can't get a grip on their obsessive-compulsive disorder. Harry felt some guilt about seeing people suffer or perceiving them as suffering. He felt he wanted to help somehow.

Chapter 12

Life as usual in Pine Creek Village

Harry had gone back to his nightly routine at the hotel. It was an absolute struggle to return on the first night back after his weekend off. Because on his two nights off of work he chose to attempt a normal life routine-this means sleeping at night and being awake in the day-he'd have a terrible time adjusting back to the graveyard shift hours when his work week re-appeared. It was *brutal*. The first day he'd be off work would feel weird. But the cruel part about it was his second night off would actually feel kind of normal. By the time Sunday morning came around, he woke up feeling good and refreshed. Problem is, by the time Sunday afternoon rolled around he'd have to somehow force himself back into bed, so he could be up all night Sunday until Monday morning to cover the desk at the hotel. Then when he got home Monday, he'd have to find a way to get enough sleep, so he could again come back Monday night at eleven p.m. in order to work until Tuesday morning seven a.m. On and on it went until it was Friday. Oh joy! This is the life of the night auditor.

Monday night was uncommonly busy for the hotel. Harry had only been able to get four hours of sleep in the afternoon yet was able to manage staying wide awake all night at work. The scientific explanation for this was that he was running on adrenaline plus several cups of coffee. Sunday night in contrast was zombie mode as he was not in any groove yet. That irritable and moody feeling in addition to the zombie mode is increasingly common for the first night back to work. But back to Monday, he'd had a couple of complaints from guests in a row. The TV channels were not coming in well enough to comfortably watch the baseball game for room 308, meanwhile the air conditioning was broken in room 150. It was a juggling act dealing with these issues because there were still people due to check in, more than usual, plus their rooms were not blocked by the previous shift. Not only were they not blocked into rooms but as Harry observed his printed-out arrivals report, he shook his head in denial about the fact that he was short on the types of rooms the folks coming in had reserved. Looking back and forth between the "all rooms available" print-out and the "arrivals" print-out he'd started to feel dizzy and tense knowing that it was another night of despair and anxiety that was much more than he wanted to deal with. You're damned if you do and you're damned if you don't he thought to himself. What can you do but just explain to the guests that you don't have what they want. If you blame the hotel and try to explain to them that it's not your fault or that it's outside of your control, then management takes it out on you assuming the guest complains. You have to remember your boss has a boss also.

The next day was another struggle for Harry. He'd still not been able to get enough rest and chalked it up to the fact that all these years attributed to a change in his sleeping patterns, which was probably causing some health issues for him. Another way to look at it is that his mind and body were finally starting to reject the backwards sleep cycle. Sure, it was never natural to begin with but finally now it was time to change. Maybe it was even God's subtle way of letting him know he needed to change.

Cassandra had emailed Harry letting him know they needed to talk. I don't like the tone of this email, Harry thought. He stepped into her office that morning, after staying an extra half hour later than usual just so he could wait for her to arrive.

"Harry, I need to talk to you about the guests in rooms 308 and what was it, oh room 150. They said you were concerned more about the time of night it was rather than helping them with their issue."

"Cassandra, the issue I have is when it comes to the air conditioning we are having a lot of trouble with the units. Sometimes they stop working all together, sometimes they just keep blowing hot air, sometimes it's cool air, sometimes the guests just want the air to completely stop but they can't get it to stop because when they turn it off, it still goes on," Harry rapidly explained.

Cassandra, exacerbated by his tone and frustration, didn't look so happy. Harry went on explaining how at say two in the morning or really any hour on the night shift for that matter, the guests just don't want to move or as we call it "transfer" to another room because they are tired and it's so late. Maybe they have a baby with them. They also typically have a ton of stuff they'd have to pack up and move. They just want the problem fixed.

"Why not offer them something for the inconvenience?" she asked.

"Sometimes I do and sometimes I don't. It's because of years of experience I know that when you try to compensate with something for the guest's problem, they can get even more angry at you if they are irate to begin with. I know, I've tried. They want the problem fixed. And it's not only that but even if they get compensated for it the next morning in some way, it's that exact moment at night that they don't want to hear any excuses, or they don't want anything other than resolution. But without the engineer on duty there is nothing that can be done *to* solve it," Harry said leaning back in his office chair.

"I want to talk to you about something more…" Cassandra continued speaking to Harry.

The conversation became more and more tense. Harry knew he was right but at the same time it was that whole *damned if you do and damned if you don't* situation at hand. The customer is always right was a policy that he didn't agree with one hundred percent. Cassandra was under pressure as usual. Harry felt both trapped by what he was being blamed for but also resentful towards Cassandra for her sexual relationship with Brandon. He knew it was wrong, but he also felt she was not only acting immoral based on work place standards but also as a person she had loose morals for jumping in the sack with Brandon and whoever else she'd had sleazy rendezvous with. He'd had enough of it and confronted her about it in a subtle enough way as not to get fired. He'd point out that Brandon was not under the same scrutiny as he was, and it was because of their *relationship*.

From the front desk, Brandon, who was on duty that morning, was able to hear voices being raised yet he wasn't able to discern what was being said as hard as he tried to listen carefully. He scratched his head and scrunched his lips together wondering what was really going on.

Chapter 13

The final days in Pine Creek Village?

Life, it was falling apart for some people. But it was coming together for others. Isn't that the way it basically always is? An interesting enigma of this existence. People die, and people are born. Some have good fortune, and some have poverty. What is fortune after all? Some don't believe in luck. The bible says God is not pleased unless we have faith. That is an interesting concept.

Harry's life was getting more and more difficult because of Cassandra's all out hatred for him, so it seemed from my vantage point. He'd been scheduled to work both overnight hours as well as daytime hours now. The justification for it, beyond the fact that we were still short staffed, was that Harry had agreed to work any shift way back when he was hired. So difficult as it was, he'd completed back to back shifts, in other words, doubles, and turn-around shifts, in other words, eight hours on, eight hours off and again eight hours on. He'd also been given extra tasks to take on such as vacuuming, dusting, organizing inside all cabinets and drawers, plus processing invoices among other things.

I have actually reached a point where I take Harry's side in the whole debacle and am willing to stand up for him. Other employees, sort of play dumb or maybe they just don't care. Beyond the fact that I'd broken the ice with him, especially that night when Sam and I visited Harry after the bar, I'd also begun to despise Cassandra. But for good reason. She was never the same in my mind after I found out she'd slept with Lex. That's just me. I know what I feel, and I can't change that. But what really got me was how she deleted those messages from Frank. Frank's a dangerous son of a bitch, there's no denying it. It's a method in life to ask around and see what people think plus use your own gut reaction. I knew enough to know that

Frank is one who I'd have to try to stay away from. But also, how good could Lex be when you put it all into consideration? Does anyone have any morals anymore?

I started to think I needed a change, but I still felt the need of Cassandra's touch paradoxically. She'd come by and walk towards me. She knew that I knew about Harry knowing about the romance between Cassandra and me. So, she was reluctant. But I looked at her straight in the eyes because I needed her. I touched her on the side at her waist. "We need to get out of here," she said. I suppose she just meant outside to get some fresh air. "Come on."

I followed her out the front door and we walked around the corner by the oak tree and wooden bench. She embraced me, and we hugged each other firmly. We stood there to cuddle for a while then kissed each other passionately. It's the intimacy that I was craving even though I knew she was not a good person.

As the days went by I learned more about Cassandra. Harry had dug up some information about her. They don't call him Harry tips and tricks for no reason. The guy knows his stuff. It turns out that on her resume she'd lied about college. In truth, she never went to college unless she did but dropped out. You can go very far in life without any formal higher education. We all can see there are very wealthy people out there who've done that, but it's another thing to lie about it. It doesn't stop there. She'd also lied about where she went to high school as well. I started to feel a bit scared of her the more I heard about her lies. I started to think she'd become like one of those femme fatales on a late night made for TV movie. Between her and the other danger I'd gotten a taste of, I realized life isn't always easy. You have to learn to avoid danger all the while still taking risks.

Chapter 14

Vacation and tragedy

Cassandra had given me something I needed the most: a vacation. I think her softer side had come through, but she still seemed to hate Harry. I savored each day of my vacation. I packed up and drove west of the river to revisit with a couple old friends and relatives. I had lunch with my mom and dad; I stayed at their place overnight. I realized that there wasn't a whole lot I missed over by my old stomping grounds, though it was nice to see family.

I wanted to get away from it all, so I remained west of the river and drove through Route Four to get to Burlington. I parked my car at the trail and walked for an hour by the Farmington River, soaking up the summer sun. I hopped back in my ride and drove down the road to Collinsville where I parked in the gravel parking lot by the antiques building. I walked past the old axe factory and could hear the rushing waterfall behind me. A few beads of sweat were slowly rolling down my face. I crossed the road and stopped to look at the fluffy dog lying down and drinking water from his bowl next to the outdoor seating at the market. I went in to order myself a hot coffee. Yes, hot coffee even when I was sweating. I rinsed my hands in the bathroom and saw a sign on the wall for open mic on Fridays.

I decided to keep going west and drove through New Hartford, Torrington and then finally I stopped in Litchfield on West Street which was the main part of town. I walked to a small local pharmacy and bought an entertainment/gossip magazine along with a cold seltzer in a glass bottle. I still had my coffee from my previous stop in the Collinsville market, so I grabbed it out of the car and walked over to the town green section and sat on a bench. Letting my thoughts dissipate, I sipped slowly on the rest of my coffee, breaking periodically to take a swig of ice-cold seltzer.

The carbonation pulsed through me and was invigorating. Birds were chirping relentlessly. I got up after ten minutes or so and tossed the empty bottle and cup in the wastebasket. Flies were buzzing all around. I turned the ignition on in my car and cranked up the AC. It was sweltering hot out there but especially in my car. I just kept driving until I passed Bantam, and then Washington. I remembered the lake out in Washington was really beautiful with some nice homes surrounding it, so I took one long loop around it. I found it eerie that a scene from a *Friday the 13th* horror flick in the 80s was actually filmed on this lake. Karen gets credit for that gem of trivia. She's into cult cinema. Interesting but not so practical bits of knowledge. That sort of thing.

Three days later….

I stopped at a coffee shop in Glastonbury on my way back to my hotel room in Pine Creek. I booted up my laptop and signed into the free wi-fi. Getting onto Facebook, I was pleasantly surprised to see a message from

Karen, my old friend and almost love interest back from the clothing store.

Our dialogue via the messenger looked like this.

Karen: Weird alert!

Brandon: What is it?

Karen: I had this dude send me a *friend request* and I accepted it. But he started asking questions that were about *you*.

Brandon: Me? what about? I want to know....

Our conversation went on while I sipped my coffee. Medium with milk only. Karen explained to me that she suspected something suspicious was going on because she could see that the guy "Greg" on Facebook had liked something connected to Jane. Jane had been buried in the back of my mind. But those memories of her and how much I wanted to be with her, those final days at the store...drinking that piping hot cherry green tea with her. That was the last time I'd seen her.

I couldn't quite make sense of how this all affected me. What would this Greg guy want to know about my relationship with Karen? Her and I were just friends. We'd kissed that one time on the couch at her on campus apartment in Hartford. Maybe it was someone not wanting me to get with her or was it someone from Pine Creek who was playing games with me? I wondered.

Brandon: Karen, I'm going to head back to Pine Creek. I miss you guys from the store. All of you.

Karen: OK drive safe, keep in touch.

Brandon: You know what, do you mind if I call you sometime? I feel like everything has changed for me so quickly that I'm still reeling from it all. You don't even know what a learning curve it's been for me out here at this hotel and some of the people I've met. Life west of the river is a lot different. Although, I've been thinking, I'm not sure which side was better.

When I was ten minutes from the hotel I got a text message on my phone. I pulled onto a quiet side road on my right and flipped my blinker on while I left the car running.

Sam: Brandon, I've got big news. Call me, lets meet for coffee at the London Fog Café or somewhere.

I rang Sam and we decided to meet up at the London Fog over in the shopping plaza. "What's going on Sam?" I asked.

He was sitting there in the back corner of the small coffee shop with a paper coffee cup in his hands sipping it, then lowered his head.

"Brandon, take a seat." The rain was falling outside. I could hear it drumming against the glass window behind Sam. I looked out at the wet landscape then thought about ordering a drink at the counter but before I could open my mouth he said, "It's Harry. He's dead."

"Excuse me," I said with my eyes wide open.

"OK, let me explain. I spoke with Lex and with Cassandra. Harry has committed suicide. He drove out somewhere and jumped off a bridge," Sam explained.

"But...."

"It's all true. They spoke to his family and he'd talked about it this past week. When you were off on vacation, they scheduled him all these crazy hours and everything was getting to him," Sam said.

We sat there for a minute more then walked out together. We passed through the hallway with that big window and the wooden bench with many sides. A large plant was growing from the center of the bench. You need plant life to make a shopping center complete if you ask me. I headed back to the hotel and spoke with Cassandra and my other coworker who was on at the time. I needed to make sense of things and piece together the loose ends.

Chapter 15

Making sense of things. Loose ends.

I knew all of what Harry complained about was true. I wished though that he could have just made some changes in his life rather than it coming to this. But he was Harry and I was Brandon. I'm not him and he's not me. I don't know what kind of issues he'd been struggling with most of his life. I still had a couple days left of vacation but of course the staff was now extremely cut short. I agreed to come back on to work tomorrow and take a rain check on the rest of my vacation. But I still had today. So, I drove out to Harry's parents' house and introduced myself as his good friend and coworker. The truth is they appreciated that I was there to talk to them because I'm glad to say I did get a chance to become at least a friend to Harry.

"Can I have this journal? I'll give it back tomorrow. I want to read what he had to say. I spoke with him in detail about everything at work and I think I can be of some help," I explained.

I don't know why they let me take the journal, but they did. I wanted to get away from the shopping plaza, the hotel and so forth. So, I drove out further to the casino. I figured I'd blow off some steam first by betting a twenty on the slot machines. I deserved it. Then I'd sit at a coffee shop somewhere out there and read what he'd had written. I sat down at a slot machine that I was more drawn to. Luckily, I had at least a twenty-dollar bill in my wallet, so I didn't have to use the ATM and get hit with double fees. I enjoyed the sounds and lights of the game. I could smell the smoke in the air subtly, but I didn't mind it. The fragrance of something pleasant was also in the air. Maybe sweetgrass and lavender or something aromatic which I couldn't place my fingers on. A song by Michelle Branch was playing in the background. The song made me feel good and something about her singing voice was youthful and vibrant. An older senior citizen had walked up to me and placed his hand on my shoulder saying, "Sometimes you gotta just glance around and do some people watching when you come here."

"Yeah, I know what you mean," I responded. In fact, the gentleman's comments were a little odd but in truth that's basically what I did everywhere I went. People watch.

I swung the lever down and watched in anticipation. The numbers, characters, symbols and such went spinning around at a rapid pace. I was down to twelve dollars in the machine. I pulled down the lever once more, betting one dollar and then it happened. I found myself looking straight ahead at three matching diamond symbols while my earnings continued to rise. I walked away with nine hundred dollars and felt elated. That nine hundred would help me out considerably.

I walked out of the casino with a smile on my face. At the car I set my GPS to a nearby Starbucks where I'd take the journal with me along with a pad and pen that I kept in the car as usual. I got in line and waited for a good five minutes. A lot was going on inside my head. I

ordered my green tea in a mug for here and
added some sugar from a couple packets, stirred
it around. I sat down and let it steep for five
minutes then added half and half and stirred it
some more with the wooden stir stick. I picked
up the mug and held it near to me while letting
the steam clear my nasal passages. It smelled
wonderful.

Reading over the journal I came across
an entry about Guy. I read it carefully. Harry
had explained how Guy was a really nice guy.
Huh… I understood how that name could cause
a person to get teased on occasion. Actually, a
name like Harry could be cause for teasing also
come to think of it. Now back to what Harry had
to write about Guy. He'd had serious issues with
obsessive compulsive disorder otherwise known
as O.C.D. along with an increase in weight that
was really bothering him. Hair loss was
affecting him as well. Guy had met up with
Harry a second time at the flea market. The first
time was the chance encounter. The second time
they'd become even better friends and went out
for a cup of coffee afterwards. On a third
occasion they were to meet up at the casino, but
Harry wasn't able to show. Harry had detailed
in his journal that he'd have to work especially

extra hours due to Cassandra making his life a living hell, basically.

I stopped to take a couple sips of my green tea, letting the piping hot water cleanse my body from the inside. I leaned back in the wooden chair. Harry continued to write about how he'd felt bad that Guy was disappointed in Harry's last-minute decision to cancel plans. Guy was struggling and in need of help. I stopped to ponder this some more.

The next day I went back to work in the morning and my mood was melancholy. Everyone was sad of course but I felt I needed to do something. A sense of purpose in my life could be to help out Guy. I after all never really fit in with the crowd. Maybe I could take over for Harry and befriend Guy. The man was probably devasted by all this. I made it through the day alright because I felt a new-found purpose in my plans to make a difference. I was cordial with all the guests in the hotel and sipped my coffee throughout the day. I took a lunch break next door at the Starlight while ordering a humus sandwich on toast. A thick slice of tomato, lettuce, cucumber on the sandwich while a side of kettle potato chips served as a nice compliment to the meal and a crunchy comfort food. I sipped a soda water through a straw on ice to wash it all down. The lunch gave me time to think.

I decided to reach out to Guy by finding him on Facebook. I got a message from him in response saying he'd be happy to meet up with me. He'd also accepted my *friend request* which made me happy. This was the start of something good.

Chapter 16

Making a difference in someone's life

I was excited and relieved to be meeting up with Guy. I was also in my hotel room, 219, sitting down and crying on the bed. I never really cry but I felt emotional over Harry and everything else. I haven't had a drink or even thought about alcohol lately, since I was so devastated by everything. Sort of a too much on my mind to have fun type of situation. I got up and drove off to meet with Guy who'd lived about 15 minutes away from Pine Creek Village.

We hit it off pretty well and I began to realize that this was the type of person I'd need in my life. An actual nice guy who could be a friend without an ulterior motive. But I also could tell that he was going through a tough time. Harry was one hundred percent correct in saying Guy struggled with O.C.D. Takes one to know one I suppose. And I knew I could help him so long as he wanted my help.

"Guy, your struggle with O.C.D. is causing you to gain weight, isn't it? I asked.

"I'm tired of the nonsense Brandon. I'm not going to hide anything anymore. It is. I'm upset over some thought, that's the obsession. I turn to food and that's the compulsion. Maybe it's because I have the thought: I need to clean the plate without leaving any food there because I don't want it to go to waste, so I eat it all. Obsession, compulsion," Guy explained.

"Maybe you're bothered by something you don't like about yourself. So, you turn to food. Your hair's falling out let's just say for example. So, you turn to food to solve that problem. Some people turn to drugs or other things," I explained. "How much do you drink Guy?"

"Well, sometimes too much."

"It's caused you to put on weight?"

"Yeah."

"You weigh how much? 300, 305?"

"Yeah," Guy responded with a look of wonder.

"I know you're wondering how I know that. I felt the same way when I was buying a treadmill oh about ten or so years ago. The guy in the store said, 'I'm not going to sell you something you don't need. Like that treadmill over there has a 700-pound capacity but you're like what, one sixty-five, right?' he said to me. I couldn't believe it but on second thought, I guess I could. It was interesting that both he and a coworker of mine also guessed my weight one time. But it made me *feel* good to know that I *was* that weight. Oh God, that coworker who guessed my weight that time was Jane. I miss her."

"I'd like to be that weight," Guy said.

"I can help you with that."

"We are about the same height, right?" Guy responded following up by also asking, "Who's Jane?"

"She's this really beautiful Japanese American woman who I worked with for years.

140

She's out in New York state now. I probably should have taken a chance on her, but I guess I didn't have the courage."

"You? Not have the courage? You look like you could be a movie star Brandon!"

"I wasn't always this way. I lost seventy-five pounds when I was a teenager. A good chunk of it first then again later when I was around college-age. I never finished school, but I've done OK for myself. My whole life changed when I got my weight to where it is now. I used to be like you; I had O.C.D. I still do. But I saw myself become more comfortable with people when I conquered my weight goal. You ever see a psychologist Guy?"

"Yeah, I don't believe in taking medications by the way, so I didn't go *that* route, but I did talk to a psychologist, yes. He'd said if things were not getting better it would be in my best interest to go see a psychiatrist to prescribe me mediations," Guy explained.

I nodded my head. "I don't believe in taking mediations either, but I don't judge anyone who does. Maybe it's the best course of action for them. But for me it wasn't something I ever wanted to do. And we have free will after all. It's a free country, right? Freedom of speech, freedom to pursue happiness."

I spoke with Guy longer than I would have even expected. We went out for a bite to eat because we were starving. I'd explained to him that the brain of someone with obsessive compulsive disorder was trained to react a certain way but with a new behavior replacing the habitual action, a healthy life would emerge. Just tell yourself that it's not your fault but you have a brain disorder that could have been inherited or caused by some type of trauma. Maybe both. Regardless. If you don't make yourself feel bad about it yet instead get excited about good changes to come, you'll be all right. You'll be better than all right. When it comes time to act out your compulsion, don't give into it. When you focus your attention on something other than your compulsion or just go about your task at hand you'll rewire your brain and major improvements will come about I told him.

"You need to decide that you're going to do whatever it takes to drop your weight and reach your goal weight," I said to Guy.

I knew that this is what he wanted because we talked endlessly, and I realized he was just like me in many ways. I told him he'd need to drop alcohol temporarily before he could drink again so that he can put a major dent in his weight loss.

"What about drinking on Fridays and Saturdays?" he asked.

I stopped to think about it for a second or two. "You know Guy, there really aren't any rules. You have to decide for yourself what you want to do."

Chapter 17

Something good is coming

One final night, that's what it would
be for Guy and me, when it came to us drinking
together. And then he'd take a break for thirty
days. Not to mention he'd weigh himself so that
he'd be able to log his progress. Sure, some
people say *throw out your scale*. But people say
a lot of things. Each and every person can do
whatever they please. In the end, the funny thing
is that when someone sees you're in shape they
want to know what you did to get that way. You
can tell them you weighed yourself seven times
a week or you could tell them you drank wheat
grass first thing every morning then did a
precise number of crunches, immediately after
jumped up and down yelling incantations.

Regardless, they're going to be drawn to what you're saying because you've got something they want. You've achieved something they're struggling with. Hence the concept of people only believing it when they see it.

We'd sat down with our pints of ale at a high, round table on bar stools. For once I got away from the Moose Pub. A good twenty minutes out of the way, we were clear of all the trouble lurking around Pine Creek Village. The bar was called The Redstone. It was eighties night, so I was relishing the music as well as some of the interesting choices in clothing. Neither of us participated in dressing to fit the decade but I at least liked glancing around the room and checking out the colorful scene. It was cool by me.

We raised our shot glasses in the air and said "Cheers," simultaneously. The spiced rum went down just fine. A little burn in the throat but a nice feeling followed.

"I've learned things the hard way at times Guy. I used to argue with people about the benefits of vegetarianism. Why tofu was a good choice. Why meat was a bad choice. But people are free to do what they'd like. I don't judge them. Take for instance this example: do you want someone telling you why you shouldn't vote for the guy you've got your heart set on voting for? You've got the bumper sticker on your car already proclaiming you're going to vote for him or her, so do you really want to argue about it? It's the same way with a lot of things," I explained.

"I've got all these diet books, cookbooks, all that stuff," Guy said.

"If I were you, I'd toss them in the garbage. But keep the cookbooks. Personally, cookbooks are a passion of mine. I like to take the meat recipes and make them vegetarian. I like the creative aspect of that. But as far as the diet books go, maybe look them over one night or however long you want to take doing it, jot down some notes that you find helpful but think about it. Calories in, calories out. Protein, Fiber, Fat, Carbs. You've got to educate yourself on the basics but too much information is more harmful than anything else at times in life. You ever hear that song by Duran Duran? *Too Much Information*. Oh well. Who would want to be educated on all this information, their mind filled to the brim but, yet they still weigh 300 plus pounds?"

"Hey! That's not nice!"

"I'm only kidding," I said.

"Hey, so am I," Guy responded.

"OK good. Tomorrow we're going to sweat like we never sweat before. Walk and jog, then uphill and downhill, and walk and jog some more. Then we'll get a good bite to eat when we're hungry. You'll have to shower before you grab that bite to eat of course. And I'll tell you what I believe. I don't believe that you have to cut out anything in your diet. You have to do what you want to do. That's why I'm kind of pissed at all those diet books. Look at it this way: if you're physically hungry, not just emotionally hungry, and you can tell the difference when you pay attention, you'll be able to burn off any type of high cal, high fat, high sugar food you put in your body. The reason why is that your body is hungry. You feel the hunger pangs. You put those calories in your system and you'll burn them off right away. Now the problem is when you put too much of them in your system. But that is one of my major lessons for you. Don't be afraid to eat what you want. And this coming from me, a vegetarian."

Our conversation flowed, and we got up for another round of beers. I enjoyed sipping and savoring the flavor. The feel of the rounded tip of the pint glass on my mouth. The scent of cologne's and perfumes in the air. The breeze as someone swooshes by you.

"I'm going to call Karen, the girl I used to work with. She's a very good artist. You should see what she does sometime," I explained while taking out my cell phone.
"Hi Brandon!"

"Karen let's talk about what you were saying before."
"You're drinking Brandon. I can tell. I'm having a drink too! Hold on...."

She got up and left the room in order to talk to me privately. Her roommate was there with her on the couch and she didn't want her to hear anything.

"I want to know more about this Facebook scenario. The guy asking about me and you," I said.

"Listen Brandon. You have to promise me something. Do you promise?"

"Yes."

"I didn't want to tell you this, but I know it's got to be Jane posing as this guy Greg. I saw her phone a long while back at the clothing store. She was out to the bank and left it behind. I looked at it to see what was on the screen. It was a Facebook account with the same Greg. It was on her screen meaning she was *logged in* as Greg. It was her account. There, I said it," Karen explained.

"OK I get it. So, you're saying she was jealous of us kissing that time. She found out somehow and she wants to know how far things got between us. And that was a long time ago too. She must really like me," I said.

"Dude, she L-I-K-E-S you *a lot*," she accentuated her words, so I got the picture. "I can tell. Women can tell. I figured as much to just give up on whatever potential *we* had together-Brandon and Karen, the Brandon and Karen that would never be- at this point especially. I'm a *little* drunk, can you tell?"

"Thank you, Karen. I think I know what I'm going to do."

"Get in touch with Jane?" Karen asked.

"Bingo. I just hope it works. At this point, I'm going to just try it. You don't know until you do," I said. Then I ended the call and put my phone down on the table.

"Well, that was refreshing. I guess the woman I really wanted all along actually likes me; she really likes me," I told Guy.

"That's great Brandon."

"Back to what we were saying. You know I really don't care for the word *lifestyle*. You know, when it comes to this whole weight loss thing, people write books and are fitness gurus, celebrities, you name it, but they are hip to not saying the word *diet*, so they exchange it for *lifestyle* or whatever other word is in vogue. But when I think *lifestyle,* I think: eat exactly this much. Don't eat this much fat, exercise three days a week, twenty minutes a day. What are we some kind of robots? You turn on the national news and you've got some doctor telling you what kind of drugs to take. Truth be told, I hate it. Why? Because they treat people like a blank slate. I can think for myself. That's why I prefer the words *mindset* or *state of mind*. You know why? Nobody can take that away from you or tell you what your state of mind is or your mindset. That's in your head. That's personal. Even when you say *in the zone*. I like that too.

"Why did you want to help me out Brandon?"

150

"I've talked with you enough to know that you care one hundred percent about being in shape. I know because I asked you all the questions I needed to, and you answered me loud and clear. Plus, you spoke up about it and expressed a desire from the bottom of your heart," I said to Guy.

"That's beautiful man but what I mean is why help me, you know what I mean? Is it because I've got a good job? You want help from me in return?" Guy asked.

"You're a computer whiz, you work from home. Technically speaking, you've got a good job. You're right about that," I explained.

"Yeah, computer whiz, works from home. That's what I put on my resume." We both laughed.

"I didn't know your job or career path in the beginning actually. You remember how I reached out to you about finding Harry's journal?" I asked.

"Yeah, sure."

"Well, obviously you know I'm devastated by Harry's death. I believe you are even more than me." I stopped to down some of my beer. "I'm going to need another one of these soon. He wrote some stuff in there about you needing help and the truth is obviously Harry needed some kind of help also. With him gone, and you here, us friends, maybe that's how we keep the candle burning so to speak. I mean maybe it all has a meaning," I said.

"So, you're really a good guy after all Brandon," Guy said.

"Let's not get too mushy here," I responded.

Chapter 18

Now it's Guy's turn

Five days later....

Guy hopped in my car and I took the back roads over to the Redstone bar once more. He flipped through my CD case and took out the *Smalltown Poets* album Jane had let me borrow. "Oh, good idea, she's on my mind as it is," I said.

"You know these guys were nominated for a Grammy back in the mid-nineties. Not for this album but even more impressive, their first album." Guy surprised me with his knowledge.

"Which category?"

"Gospel, Christian-contemporary, something like that," he'd said.

"What? They're a Christian rock band?"

"Yeah, you couldn't figure that out?"

"No, I hardly listened to it." I stopped talking for a few seconds to let it sink in and coasted down the road. "So that's why Jane wanted me to borrow this album. Maybe it was her subtle way of letting me know she wanted a Christian guy, or regardless I'm glad you told me this stuff Guy."

We parked the car then walked in the front entrance. I turned my head back and reached out my right arm, touching him on the shoulder. "Remember you're only having…"

"I know, *Ice water*, and that's cool."

"This is your time to see serious progress. Thirty days with no alcohol. And the way you're eating. Cutting your calories, it's going to show. I can already see the difference," I said.

We found a table and sat down. "I want to thank you for helping me out Brandon. You don't know what I've been through over the years," he'd said.

"I think I do. I've been there too. You should have seen me. When you lose seventy-five pounds you're not the same person really. *I* wasn't anyways. You think that it's not going to change your personality? You go from always wanting a girl in your life and never having a chance until one day you finally figure it all out." I stopped talking and snapped my fingers in front of me. "It all clicks and presto, you're at an ideal weight. I can't speak for everyone, but I got a lot of attention. Hey, maybe it wasn't even much attention but when you go from nothing to something, relatively speaking, you notice it. All of a sudden some of the most beautiful girls were looking at me in a way that I never thought would be possible. You think that's not going to cause someone to have ego problems after years of neglect? Not just neglect from the opposite sex but being ostracized from friends in general for some amount of years. You're going to become arrogant or something else. Until you learn better. So, look out Guy because your life is going to change when you look about half your size," I said.

He nodded his head and listened.

"I'm going to order myself a shot. Give me a minute," I said.

"I'll be here with my ice water," Guy Said.

I came back to the table with a tequila shot, some salt and a lime wedge. "I've got an extra lime wedge. You want it?"

"Yeah sure."

"Here goes nothing." I licked the salt off the side of my hand. Down the chute. I bit into the lime wedge lastly. "Oh, that was nice," I said wiping my mouth with the back of my hand and placing the shot glass on the counter.

"You really think I can do it?" Guy asked.

"Loose the weight, reach your goal?"

"Yeah."

"I don't believe you can do it. I know you can do it," I said with conviction.

"You know you see people sometimes looking sad and you say to yourself: I would just die to be with her, she's so beautiful. Like this one woman I saw looking sullen. Maybe other guys wouldn't think twice about her, but beauty is in the eye of the beholder," Guy said.

"I think I get what you're saying," I responded.

"Well you just wonder how people feel about themselves. Like it could be anyone going through a hard time and you wonder how much of that is them having low self-esteem. But if they knew how valuable they are in the eyes of some other people...complete strangers even, then they would feel better, you know what I mean?" Guy said.

"Yeah I agree totally. It's like when you're out say at the mall and walking by a store. You might see a female working there out of the corner of your eye but to her she could think you're the most gorgeous man on the planet or she just might feel something for you. I don't know. How do you know? You walk by and glance at someone else. You can't interpret every single person around you. You're not a mind reader, you're not God," I said. "So, you wonder sometimes about missed opportunities."

"You know the vegetarian diet you're on. I've been thinking about it a lot. The original theory is that, according to the Judeo-

Christian faith, man, and all animals were vegetarian. In the book of Genesis God created all things good so there was no death and suffering hence the vegetarian diet. It wasn't until after the flood, Noah's flood, that God permitted man to eat animals, Genesis 9:3 if you want to get specific."

"I never knew that Guy. But I'm surprised you know this. You didn't strike me as the religious type," I said.

"How do you think I knew that *Smalltown Poets* CD was Christian? I also subscribe to *Creation Magazine*. I got a box set of DVDs' explaining the science of Creation and I just love this older book I got in the mail last month: *Doubts about Creation? Not After This!* Yeah, I know it's not the most popular view out there these days, but I believe in Creationism. There's no other way to make sense of the bible. Not without throwing out the whole genealogy of Jesus, not to mention all types of evidence out there adds up to backing this view," Guy explained.

"Listen Guy, I'm going to make a phone call to Jane but it's a little loud in here. Will you excuse me?"

I walked down the corridor and around the corner. The bar had this lobby or waiting room so to speak. I don't know what it was, but it had a comfortable black leather couch, so I just sat down on it and dialed Jane.

"Brandon?"

"Yes, it's me."

"I haven't heard from you in forever," Jane responded.

"Well, I hope you don't mind but I'm having a drink while I talk to you. Actually, my drink is on the table with Guy but if I sound a little affected you know why," I explained.

"Which Guy?"

"His name is Guy."

"Oh OK! I like that name," she responded.

"You know? I do too. So how is Rhinebeck?" I asked.

"Oh, it's not Avon, Connecticut, but it's not bad. I guess I just feel like I've been thrust into a whole new world out here. I've been really considering my future Brandon. How is everything going for *you*?" Jane asked.

"Oh, it's been exciting. I'm working out at a hotel in this small-town east of the river. Things have gotten a little crazy shall we say. I'll spare you the details," I explained.

"A hotel?"

"Yeah, it's a good learning experience. It's a lot more complicated than I thought it would be. You do learn a lot." There was a pause in our conversation for a few seconds.

"I want to tell you something," we both said it simultaneously.

"Wow," I interjected.

"Yeah, wow… you go first," Jane responded.

"OK well, I suppose I should tell you this beforehand. Yesterday I was at a funeral."

"A funeral?"

"Yes, a guy named Harry. It was a suicide."

"Friend of yours? A coworker?"

"Yeah, he was at the hotel. Worked night audit for too many years."

"I'm sorry Brandon. Maybe you need to get out of there."

"I think I'm about ready to head back west of the river. Find something new to do with my life. But what I was going to say was, would you like to go out to dinner with me?" The hell with going out for coffee I thought. I wanted her to know I was serious. Life is short. I want to be clear this would be a date. A glass of red wine. Fancy table cloth. I'll order a pasta primavera or something like that. She'll order whatever she wants to order. I'll offer to pay for the date. The old-fashioned way. Because I'm starting to gather, she's the old-fashioned type.

"I'd love to Brandon."

"What were you going to say before when you had something to tell me?" I asked her.

"Oh, I'll save that for dinner. It's nothing really; it just will give me something to talk about with you."

After finishing up my phone call with Jane, I walked back to the bar and apologized to Guy for ditching him for a bit. "Good thing you're not drinking anything except water. Way to go. Now let's get out of here. Whattaya say?"

"Good, I was getting bored drinking this ice water for so long."

Chapter 19

Things are going to change

I was nervous and excited about my date with Jane. I called her back the next day to finalize plans just like we discussed we would.

"Jane, I'd like to meet at Stamford Town Center.... would that be ok with you?" I asked.

"Hmmm yes, actually Stamford Mall is where they filmed part of *Scenes from a Mall*, back in the early nineties. You know, that Woody Allen flick," she said. "Did you know that?"

"Yeah actually, believe it or not, I *did* know that," I responded.

"And it's about roughly a half-way point for us. Well let's face it Brandon, I don't know where you are, Pine Valley? Pine Creek, Pine Woods? Something like that but it's somewhere out there in the eastern side of the state so it must be at least an hour, probably closer to approaching a two-hour drive depending on traffic," Jane said.

"Well listen Jane, I hope it's OK I bring my friend Guy along," I said.

"Absolutely."

Guy and I got in his SUV and he immediately turned up the AC. Beads of sweat were pouring down his face. He took a roll of paper towels from the back seat and dried himself off. He had a collection of CDs in a small booklet that held about a dozen.

"Pick out something Brando!" He called me by a nickname I rarely heard from anyone, but it was OK with me.

I saw a collection of mostly smooth jazz music. *Boney James*, the album *Ride*. *Boney James*, *Pure*. *Jon B Cool Relax*. I took out the *Jon B.* CD and inserted it.

"I never really *heard* the man's music, but I'd always wanted to buy this CD back when I was in high school. I don't know why. Maybe because the album title: "Cool Relax" just intrigued me. Boney James, well Boney, I've been a fan of for a long time myself. I hear that he got his name Boney from being on tour earlier in his career over in one of the Scandinavian countries in northern Europe. Everything was so damn expensive out there; he said he wouldn't be able to afford to eat much and eventually he'd get *boney*. So, the name stuck and probably was a bit catchier and more marketable than his birth name: James Oppenheim," I explained.

It became quite noticeably cooler in the SUV as ten to fifteen minutes had passed. I looked over at Guy and I could see he looked happy. I felt like I was doing my part by helping him to make his dreams come true. He really was the bridge between Harry and me. It was all just too weird. The way things happened. The whole chain of events, if you will.

"This is a far drive huh?" Guy said. "But I don't mind."

"I want to take you here because, I don't know about you, but I get inspired when I go to malls. Just think Guy, when you look around the stores like say Abercrombie and Fitch or say Aéropostale-they don't have my old store there by the way-shut down five years ago in Stamford, kinda sad but now I'm getting off topic. But you get excited about clothes when you've gone from being the fat kid to Mr. GQ. Maybe other people who haven't had that transformative experience enjoy it just the same. I don't really know."

"It's exciting. I'm going to make it up to you Brandon. The way you're helping me out."

"Maybe you're helping me out more than I'm helping you," I said.

We didn't say anything for a while and just drove. I felt the cool breeze of the air conditioning soothe my skin. It felt like a refreshing dip in a backyard inground pool on a scorching summer day. I just gazed out the window while I listened to the tunes.

"I need to get some gas. You mind if I stop at the next exit?" We were already on Route 8 South and hit that scenic valley region around the small town of Beacon Falls. I got out of the car to stretch my legs.

"You want some money for gas?" I asked.

"Oh no, I'm good."

I went inside the store and browsed around. Spearmint gum, why not? Soda…mmm, no. Hot coffee, nah I need to cool off. People magazine and an iced vanilla latte drink looked appealing to me. That's what I decided on. It was one of those fancy automatic iced coffee drink creation stations where you made it yourself by putting the clear plastic cup underneath and pressing a button. Of course, first you'd fill it with ice. I grabbed a straw and a few napkins, paid the cashier, turned around and pushed the door open with my backside. I noticed Guy closing up the gas tank.

"Ready to go bud?" I asked with a hint of enthusiasm in my voice.

"You got it!"

We got back in the car and the grooves started playing as he turned the ignition on. "What time is your date?" he asked.

"We made 5:15 reservations for this nice modern Italian place right outside the mall. I figure you can just walk around while we're doing dinner. If you want to eat, I recommend you get a falafel wrap with a soda water on ice at the food court. That is if you want to go the vegetarian route. Otherwise have whatever you want. Knock yourself out!"

The traffic got intense. I could see Guy focusing on it. I was just thankful it wasn't me driving. My thoughts drifted away, and I fell into a kind of zone listening to the music and looking out the window while we zoomed by countless trees.

"Get off this exit, Atlantic Street. Pull into where it says, "Mall Parking." We're actually going to pay for parking, but they make it really easy these days. You pay with your credit card and the ticket prints out telling you when your time expires."

We walked in at the food court and took the escalator up one more level. Guy glanced around and said, "This is kind of like Westfarms Mall but in a sense it's really kinda different too." He studied the geometric pattern of the mall's layout. We got to the top of the escalator and glanced over the railings. "These things make me a little worried. Look down there. You've got that seating area in red. It's like a row of steps going in every direction but everyone's just kinda sitting there and hanging out," he said.

"Personally, I like it. I like that fountain down there, way at the bottom. This is the top level, so basically, it's an art exhibit. Just these cool paintings are all you'll find." We walked around the perimeter and studied the works. "Interesting, sexy…realism, abstraction all on the same canvas…subtle brushstrokes." You could tell each piece went together as a series which was an important sign of an artist using the organizational power of his mind. "Ready to go down?" I asked.

Once we descended a couple more levels, we just got in a groove and kept talking. I could appreciate the fact that we both walked at the same pace. I slowed down to match his rate. There's nothing more aggravating than walking with someone who's always five or ten steps ahead of you. I was more of an introspective person so walking slower to talk about life was my type of thing. It was also more relaxing that way.

"You know, I remember the old times," I began to say. Guy listened on. "Like back in the late nineties. I was in high school, had my

license at this point. I had this friend who'd
hang out with me every now and then. We'd
seen a concert once, gone out shooting pool at
least a couple times. He'd lived on the other side
of town. So, I suppose it was the advantage of
having a car at that age which sort of bridged
the gap between students who never knew each
other in their youth because they grew up on
opposite sides of town. But this kid was nice, a
little different, because he'd had a quality I'd
noticed. He'd never been one to boast or argue
with you. And that's rare but in a good way. So,
we were out at a mall about half an hour from
our town, just to explore a further away place. I
think we had this in common: we liked
exploring other places out there, even driving to
get lost purposely at times. We'd been at the
mall walking around then decided on seeing a
movie down the street. This was before the time
that people had GPS devices, so we'd just
wanted to ask for directions. I remember one of
us asked this guy who worked at the mall, but
he'd had a hard time talking to us because he
was having a panic attack I suppose. I don't
know exactly what It was, but I felt for the guy.
We just both listened to him and he helped give
us directions. I always remembered that moment
because there was something about it. I think
about how many times I've been judged or

picked on when I was a kid. I know you've probably been there too Guy."

"I've been there too, you're right. Guy said then looked down at his shoes to check the laces. We continued to walk through the mall. A Starbucks was on our right. I eyed it for a moment, but our conversation was going so well I didn't want to interrupt the flow of it. "There was this old memory I had that came to me the other day. I was watching TV, I don't know how many years ago, and I saw Richard Simmons, you know that *sweatin' to the oldies* guy, talking to a lady, she was likely rather heavy I remember, and she was kind of emotional when she told Richard this, but she'd said she was out with friends and they were all eating ice cream, but she'd ordered an ice water. It makes me think about sacrifice and that good things don't come easy. It's like that compassion you're talking about Brandon. To respect other people and not just turn what other people do or say into folly. You know in the book of Proverbs it says, 'He will humiliate those who make fun of others, but he will honor those who humble themselves.' Isn't that a good message?"

"That's a beautiful message Guy."

"What was it that got you to lose all that weight in the first place Brandon?"

"Truth is Guy...there's personal stuff that got in the way to begin with. Stuff that prevented me from losing weight. Something I don't want to get into right now. But when I resolved it...I noticed a brochure for the Soloflex. You know, that one piece of fitness equipment which allowed you to work your entire body from head to toe? I never bought one. They weren't very popular at that time. Sure, I'd love one regardless of how outdated they might have seemed at the time, but I settled on a newer piece of equipment that was only half as good I'm sure. It cost less as well. It was also before the time of the Bowflex, keep in mind. But that brochure from the Soloflex really educated me on the benefits of weight training. It laid it all out in bullet form: Strength training increases your metabolism and it went into detail, for those much older it would be a way of preventing bone loss, burning fat, makes you look younger, feel younger, the list went on. I'm paraphrasing here of course. I was convinced so I just got to work on eating less and working out more. I had a membership to the YMCA as well," I said.

"I saw this commercial Brandon, it was for a running magazine, also back in the nineties I think. They said something that really stuck with me. If you're a runner you need to get this magazine, if you've even been thinking about starting to run you should get this magazine. Something to that effect. I felt like this was good advertising because I wasn't a runner and I was and am grossly overweight, hopelessly overweight but here was this running magazine telling me that I should get a subscription even If I was obese and never ran in my life. It made me feel good," Guy said.

"It's like that with the exercise equipment infomercials. I used to love those because they also made me feel good, really good. Like sure they want to sell you the piece of equipment, so they set it in a beautiful room in the house with nice big windows. Everything is sparkling clean. But why not let that *inspire* you? Why not buy that equipment and put it in the nice room of the house? Why not let it motivate you to keep your place clean. I'd think to myself Guy, back in those days, when my workout was finished it was like *all was well with the world*. I actually heard a guy say those words on a commercial advertising the equipment, but it was so true. And ever since I got myself in shape, it's been like looking at the world through rose colored glasses. But you know, people don't want to hear that. People are too damn cynical out there! But people also don't want to live the life that I lived *prior* to being in shape and all that I'd been through. It's the contrast, the difference between the before and after. You can't tell someone how *they* feel. You're not inside their mind," I said.

"That's deep Brandon."

"Keep your phone on. It's five. I'm going to meet up with Jane now."

"Are you going to tell her my idea?"

"No, listen. She's going to think I'm crazy," I said.

"Yeah but it's what you want in life and…." he began to say.

"I know but…let's just see how things go." I walked away and headed to the lower level exit.

I met Jane outside the restaurant. She stood there pacing around just a little wearing a white open front cardigan over a blue and white dress with an intricate pattern. The dress went down to about the knee length and she wore a pair of brown loafers.

"Hi Jane."

"Hi, how are you?"

"I'm glad to see you."

"So am I."

We paused for a moment and I thought about whether to give her a hug or not. It didn't seem right at the moment, so I stood there for a second and glanced around. "They're calling us now. Our table must be ready."

We were seated and like I predicted we both wanted to order red wine. I had recognized this wine on the list called Toad Hollow from California. The cabernet sauvignon had a hint of cherry, plum and dark chocolate flavors with a scent of white pepper and cedar. She said she couldn't wait to try it.

"Jane, I never realized how good that CD was you let me borrow. *Smalltown Poets* are amazing. The singer has an incredible voice."

"Thank you, Brandon. I want you to know that this evening has been a real blessing for me because my life has been a little hectic out there in Rhinebeck with the store and all. I'm just looking for a change you know? And when you called, it was like wham! Just what I needed."

"What was it that you were going to say that time on the phone when I called you from the bar? Remember when we both said, *I want to tell you something* at the same exact moment?" I asked.

"Oh yes, well what I wanted to say to you was…this is kind of embarrassing… the same as you wanted to say to me, which essentially was: *Would you like to go out for dinner?"* she said.

"That's beautiful Jane."

"Seriously Brandon, you don't know how many times I thought about you since the store closed down in Avon."

"I've thought about you too Jane. I just never really believed that we'd be a reality."

"And I never thought we'd be either. I mean there is 1) the fact that I was your boss and 2) you had just about every woman who walked into our store look at you like you were on the menu. And let's be honest here, you did go out with a handful of them," she said with a smile.

I hesitated and let out a small sigh then looked down at the table. The waiter arrived and served us our wine, pouring it in our glasses. In the corner of my eye I saw the glowing string of white lights up in the distance splayed about giving this establishment a pleasant ambience. I brought the glass to my nose and inhaled slightly. She looked into my eyes right after. I looked back and felt a sensation inside me. In my mind I thought: *damn, she is beautiful*. Next, I thought: *this is really happening*. Our food came to the table and I had the pasta primavera with spaghetti in a rich cream sauce flavored by a blend of sharp cheeses and garlic, with carrots, peas, broccoli, squash, and roasted onions. She had the chicken marsala. We shared a house salad along with the soft fresh bread and butter on the side. The food was delectable, but her phone went off after a couple minutes into our dinner.

"I don't mind if you take the call Jane."

"OK thanks, it's "Spontaneous Lauren.""

Who, I thought.

"Hello Lauren. I'm having dinner now…."

She put the phone down on the table. "Will you excuse me Brandon? She says it's an emergency."

"Sure of course"

"I won't be long."

She got up and left for a few minutes. I sat back in my chair and put my hands behind my head. I'd take a break from eating my food. Next, I picked up my glass and took a good long slow sip of the wine, savoring the flavor.

She returned to the table at a hurried pace. "Sorry."

"No don't worry about it, that was pretty quick."

"My friend Lauren…."

"You called her *spontaneous* Lauren."

"Yeah, anyone else would've called her *crazy* Lauren or *something like that,* but you know me," she lowered her voice when she said it. "But yes, she's coming up with new and spontaneous ideas. Like let's go out for coffee right now! She'd say this even though its nine p.m. and I'd tell her all the coffee shops are closed but she'd find somewhere, and we'd talk about life and stuff. She was definitely eccentric, I'd say that."

"So, what's the emergency? No wait, that's probably personal," I said.

"Well listen Brandon. Here's the thing. I need a change in my life. We seem to be getting along well. I wouldn't ordinarily say something like this, but I feel chemistry between us and look, I've been living my life on the straight and narrow for so many years. It's now or never. And it's not like I don't know you. I worked with you for years. How would you feel about continuing dating but if we did so we'd have to live closer together?" She asked.

"Are you thinking about moving out of Rhinebeck?... Or are you asking me to move there?"

"OK that's where spontaneous Lauren comes in. She knows how you have this dream of packing up and moving to the middle of the country: Nebraska. So, she wants me to propose this question to you: would you take a road trip out there and see how things go? Whatever happens, happens. We wouldn't room together because that's not something that I believe in doing before marriage. Ok there I said it. But it was Lauren's idea and I figured you'd said you wanted to leave that Pine Creek place after all," Jane said then exhaled a sigh.

"Listen Jane, you're not going to believe this but my friend Guy, who's here inside the mall, you'll meet him afterwards, has suggested the same exact idea Lauren had for us. He tried to convince me to drop this idea on you, but I told him you'd think I was cuckoo for cocoa puffs," I said with a straight face and then she started laughing. I also laughed a bit at that point.

"So, what do you say?" she asked.

"I think it's perfect. Guy wants to be my roommate. I also want to be his roommate, so it works out. We'll have a hell of a time and it will be our big adventure. Plus, if someone calls us crazy, they'll have to call all four of us crazy," I said.

"Let's get crazy Brandon."

We finished our food while talking about a variety of things. "Listen Jane, I realize that you're a Christian and I think I'd like to give that a try. I want to do what I have to do to be on board with this whole thing. I mean, talk about a blessing. I end up with you and you're

180

the one who's doing things the right way. Who else would I want to be with? Someone with loose morals? I always wanted you all along."

"Let's take it one day at a time. And I'm going to savor each and every one of those days too. We'll get to know each other, and, in the end, we'll know whether it was just friendship and one big adventure or whether it was something much more. But I have a feeling it's romance because when you feel it you know it." She took her left hand and placed it on top of my right hand and I felt the warmth of her palm and fingers on me.

A little bit later I introduced Guy to Jane and she called Lauren up at that point and passed the phone around to each of us, so we could briefly talk to this wild and wonderful lady. We were thrilled about our next step in life and all promised each other we'd follow through with it and never back out. I'd wanted to do the right thing and give two-weeks' notice at the hotel in Pine Creek Village. I wanted to say goodbye to Cassandra and my other coworkers. I wanted to say bye to the other cast of characters living out there and tell them thank you for the time they'd spent with me. Well maybe not all of them but my time there is something I'd never forget.

I talked to Guy that evening after the mall. We'd had a good long drive back after all. He and I conversed about the route we'd take to Nebraska and how much we'd pack for the trip. And the four of us had exchanged contact information earlier to make this journey a reality. "You know Guy, I don't know what it is, but I often wanted to be somewhere other than where I was in life. I felt it during middle school and high school. Going to this Pine Creek Village was different, I'll give it that, but it wasn't exactly where I'd belong either. Still it was part of the journey. It was necessary for the chain of events now that I think about it. Years ago, I'd sometimes get this feeling when I'd go out cruising through Connecticut and stop at some random gas station, especially if it was twilight. I'd get this feeling like I was in a fresh new place. Somewhere different from home. Somewhere simpler. I don't know. I just got these feelings or vibes. You know like when you see a day time reality-based TV talk show type of thing and they are filming out somewhere in a different state and you say to yourself, I don't know what it is but maybe I belong there? Well this journey we're taking has been thirty some years in the making so however it ends at least we're putting it into motion…making it a reality," I said.

"We're making something happen Brandon. Yes, we are. And let's not forget about Harry. Let's do it in his honor."

About the Author

Adam Kovynia is a first-generation American, born in 1981, in New Britain, Connecticut. He moved to Southington, Connecticut at age four and attended public schools and later graduated from Paier College of Art with a bachelor's degree in Illustration in 2003. He enjoys reading books at coffee shops throughout the nutmeg state, music and movies, especially of the 1980s and 90s, and sampling fine quality coffee, beer or rum. Some of his most memorable vacation experiences include anywhere in Florida, but especially Disney World, Poland, England, Vermont and the Creation Museum in Kentucky. He enjoys vegetarian cooking, massage, and learning new ways of understanding life. Adam is single and lives in Connecticut but thinks about moving to a new state in the not too distant future. *Brandon's Journey East and West* is his second book. *Max's Modern-Day Philosophy* is his first.